Stones of Sandhill Island

by

Peggy Chambers

Sandhill Island Series

Stones of Sandhill Island

Cover Art by *Kim Mendoza*

The Wild Rose Press, Inc.
PO Box 708
Adams Basin, NY 14410-0708
Visit us at www.thewildrosepress.com

Publishing History
First Mainstream Mystery Edition, 2018
Print ISBN 978-1-5092-1892-9
Digital ISBN 978-1-5092-1893-6

Sandhill Island Series
Published in the United States of America

There were letters,

ribbons, and programs from evenings at the ballet. Her mother's memories, and Billie felt the stab of pain once again. Her mother's entire life in one box on the bed. How would she get through this again?

The pale blue padded envelope lay in the bottom. She gently lifted the lip, and the edges of the paper crumbled in her hands. Inside she found a note written in heavy scrawl, and a black book of matches with gold filigree letters told of bygone days when all the best clubs gave out matchbooks to their patrons. *Johnny Fats*, it read, and she flipped open the cover. The matches were dry and probably still worked. She laid them aside and read the letter.

"My dear Giselle," it read. *"I will never forget the night we met, and I await your answer."*

No signature. Her mother must have known who sent it, or she would not have kept it all these years.

Her mother always said that Billie's father was a dancer who could not marry her. She said no more whenever Billie brought it up. Could he have been the man who sent the note, and if so, what answer did he await? She would never know. Why did she wait so long to open the box, and why the big secret? She and her mother had a beautiful life together, so what did it matter? But she wanted to know.

She fingered the matches as her heart once again ached. It felt like a new cut on top of an old wound that still had not fully healed. And the infection bubbled to the surface.

Praise for Peggy Chambers

"Peggy Chambers writes like most of us dream. Her *SECRETS OF SANDHILL ISLAND* is a definite must-read from cover to cover. Full of mystery, romance, and absolute character development, lost loves and loves found. You won't just want to read, you'll want to absorb, you'll want more...much, much more. Can't wait for the next in the series."

~*Gerry Christina, The Writer's Block, LA Talk Radio*

Acknowledgments

Many thanks go out to County Judge Danny L. Chambers and County Attorney Andrew Lucas of Somervell County, Texas, for their assistance in understanding the Texas Victim Compensation Fund, and other legalities in small-town Texas.

I am also deeply appreciative of the professional opinion and work done regarding the psychological aspects of the book by Brandi Gibson, LMFT, LADC. She was a great help in reviewing the scenes involving Billie and her psychologist in this work of fiction.

Prologue

Two years earlier

Squealing tires and screeching metal-on-metal shredded Billie's eardrums.

In the backseat, right behind his dad, Jimmy sang the song again. The one that Billie thought would drive her crazy. But Jimmy loved it, so she tried to.

Temporarily blinded by oncoming light, she turned to look at her son, when she saw the other vehicle veering into their lane. Swerving to avoid the head-on collision, Steve took the brunt of the impact on his side—not hers. Glass crushed in on the driver's side and air bags deployed. Side impact steel bars bent inward as the van rolled on its side. Billie's head pounded the door each time it rolled over—she had no idea how many times—and the glass on her side never broke. The driver's side—not so lucky.

She awoke in a night so dark she thought she lay inside a coffin. No light. No air. The humidity of the summer night clawed at her throat as she tried to breathe. She opened her mouth to scream but nothing came out. She wanted to see her son, but a blanket of dark kept her from seeing outside its boundaries. Once again, she passed out.

She woke the second time to flashing lights and sirens. Billie had no idea how long she lay there shrouded in darkness, but she knew one thing; she hurt all over. Proof of life. Her chest felt crushed from the seatbelt, and her face was bruised by the air bags. Again, she tried to scream, anything, a name. "Jimmy!" It came out like a dandelion puff. And darkness again.

More screeching metal, and suddenly a light in her eyes and hands on her body, lifting her gently onto a stretcher, then whisking her away with sirens.

When she again regained consciousness, she found the pain gone, and her foggy head began to clear. Where was her husband?

Where was her son? The boy had been named for his paternal grandfather, James Stone, Steve's father, whom he had never met. And now he never would.

Chapter 1

Present day

Balance. According to the therapist, Billie needed to achieve balance between her spiritual and physical life—and balance between her social and private life. Meditation could be the vehicle to get her there if practiced well.

Perched one on top of the other and rocking in the breeze, the smooth wet stones glowed in the filtered sunlight. Waves crashed on the shore and mist brushed her cheek as she let go of the top-most pebble. It wiggled slightly, then tumbled as a gust blew up from the sea scattering the entire tower of rocks onto the sand at her bare feet.

She'd try again tomorrow. She breathed deeply. Maybe some different stones. The tide would come in and take these anyway. Life was like that. Here today and gone tomorrow—she should know. But now she needed a shower. She needed to fix dinner for her mother, Giselle, and then get ready for her set at Le Chez. Maybe the diners would enjoy a little Janis Joplin tonight since the piano would be set up outside. The raspy voice of Janis could get a little noisy in a small restaurant. There wasn't room for a jazz singer with a microphone, so they moved her outside when they could.

Rising, she picked up the yoga mat and rolled it, placing it in the bag with the iPod and ear buds. She almost never listened to music when she meditated and balanced rocks. The sound of the ocean set her mind free. She listened to spa music for her yoga practice. The fishermen who sometimes came down to the rocks looked at her strangely at first, but soon got used to the figure of the dark-haired woman, barefoot in yoga pants, sometimes playing with rocks like a child on the shore.

But she was not a child and she had responsibilities—like a job, and her mother. Billie had grown up on the tiny strand made mostly of sand aptly named Sandhill Island many years ago. One end of the island—the one she loved best—she found rocky and mysterious with blue-green water foaming over rocks then pulling back out to sea. Her breathing synced with the never-ending back and forth of the water. She couldn't believe she'd ever lived anywhere else. Why would she? But she knew why. There were no night clubs for singers on the tiny island except during the tourist season, which was never long enough. But now back to heal, and to help her mother heal as well, she would do her best.

Slipping into flip-flops she walked the short distance toward her mother's weather-beaten home. It needed repairs. The wind and salt were relentless. Paint could be stripped in a season if the storms were frequent, and washing salt-encrusted windows was an almost constant chore, something she needed to do again. She kept her mother's bedroom window clean, so the ailing woman could look out to sea. Mom had so few good things in her life these days.

4

Billie stopped by the post office in town before heading home. She often forgot to check the mail, used to home-delivery when she lived in Corpus Christi. But Sandhill Island was not a normal town. The ferry, the only way back and forth to the mainland, made the postal area necessary. Each home had a box at a central location instead of on their own porches.

She kept the key to the mail box in the tiny pocket of her yoga pants. Inserting it into the keyhole, she found a few bills, magazines, and a notecard addressed to her with a return address of Keesler AFB. She knew only one person at Keesler.

Maj. Sandra Miller was her oldest friend from high school. The jazz singer and the scientist made an odd mix, but they spent a lot of time together when they were younger. Then Sandy went off to college to become a meteorologist, followed by joining the Air Force, marrying, and having two kids. Billie moved to Corpus Christi and the limelight to follow her dreams on stage. Sandy saw the world, while Billie saw the Gulf of Mexico from a larger city than the one she grew up in. Sandy had two children while Billie had none—not anymore.

She opened the door to her mother's residence. No key needed. They never locked the door on the island, unlike Billie had in Corpus. It was also her home—something Billie reminded herself of over and over. She grew up in this house. Then she became an adult and moved away. Now that she was back, it had once again become her home; her mother told her that, and Billie tried to remember.

"I'm home," Billie called out.

"Your mother is such a dear." Raven stood in the

doorway to the kitchen in scrubs with her dark hair pulled back in a French braid. Jamaican born, she studied nursing and moved to Corpus Christi. The home healthcare group she worked for assigned her to Giselle Martin on Sandhill Island. Raven was well suited to island life. She came in five days a week and worked her schedule around Billie's. That way Billie's mother, Giselle, never stayed alone. She helped with the cooking and cleaning along with health care and bathing Giselle. Billie knew the domestic chores were not in her job description, but the nurse did the things necessary for her patient. Giselle had Parkinson's, a painful and debilitating disease, and Billie watched her mother live with it daily.

When the car accident happened two years ago, Billie came back home to visit and heal, only to find her mother falling on painful legs. Then the tremors started, and Billie knew her mother needed help. Billie was not the only one who knew pain. They found the diagnosis of Parkinson's devastating, maybe even more painful than the disease itself. Giselle was a beautiful, vibrant woman and more determined to help her daughter heal than herself. Her health problems were put on the back burner until the diagnosis came. Then they had to trade roles.

"Yes, she is. What did she do this time?" Billie placed the mail on the antique buffet and pulled a letter opener from the top drawer, slicing the envelope open, excited to see what her friend had to say.

"You know she's having trouble swallowing her food, so I started putting it in a blender or mashing it up for her. Well, today she wanted an apple, and I mashed it. She told me she used to put allspice on it for you and you would eat it right up. I sprinkled some on her apple, and she insisted I try it too. She said it could be used as an anti-oxidant, and with nursing, I might be exposed to disease. Like I could catch what she has. But she is a dear. And apples are better with the spice on it. I'm surprised my mama didn't do that when we were kids. But we didn't have an apple tree in Jamaica, just citrus. We didn't eat many apples."

Billie no longer listened as she read Sandy's note. Now that there was email, no one wrote letters anymore, but Sandy was old fashioned like Billie. Part of why they were such good friends. The note held pictures of her and her kids on the beach playing in the waves. She loved Sandy, and the kids made her heart ache for her own. The tragic car accident that took the lives of her son and husband left her untouched—at least physically. Late one Friday evening on the Crosstown Freeway, they met Joe Franks heading the wrong way. The accident, over in a second, would last a lifetime for Billie. The therapist told her that she would not get over her husband and son's deaths but learn to live with them. For Billie, it would be a life-long learning process.

The note said Sandy and the kids were coming for Spring Break and wanted to see Billie while on the island. Sandy wanted some time with her children before hurricane season hit and she got busy.

"Billie?" Mom's soft voice called from the bedroom where she spent most of her time these days.

"Coming, Mom." Billie put the card on the buffet with the rest of the mail and walked across the hall to her mother's room. She had placed her mother in the room with the most available light. The doctors said depression was part of the problem with Parkinson's patients, and light therapy helped. Billie knew a lot about depression.

"What's the weather like?" Giselle sat in the wheel chair looking out to sea, her legs mostly useless these days. Her pale blue robe and slippers accentuated clear blue eyes and silver hair pulled back in a neat bun at the back of her head. Tiny wisps of curls escaped the pins that held the rest and framed her face. Though aging, Giselle still had a beauty that belied her age. A southern belle, she had lived her life in the Corpus Christi and Sandhill Island area, and her mother had named her Giselle after the ballet.

"Warm and a little windy. It blew over the stones I stacked. But they were small." Billie smiled at the woman who raised her and then took her in again when tragedy struck.

"Are the ones on the porch still standing?" Giselle used to watch Billie as she practiced her daily ritual of mediation, stacking the stones on top of each other. Some larger ones still sat on the porch, and Billie often rolled her mother's chair out to see them and enjoy the sea air. For some reason, the older woman loved the stacked stones too. Billie thought of the simple act as meditation for both of them.

"Yeah, they're too big to blow over unless there is a storm. Speaking of storms, Sandy is coming. She sent a card that she is bringing the kids to the island during Spring Break and I can't wait to see them."

"I'm sure they have grown a foot." Giselle folded the robe on her lap with gnarled fingers.

"Oh, you know it. Full of vim and vigor I'm sure."

"And how will you handle that?" Giselle looked

into her daughter's eyes. Parkinson's, a disease caused by a loss of dopamine producing cells in the brain, had not dulled her emotions. She still thought of others first.

"I'll smile and enjoy them." Her mother still worried about her. The feeling was mutual these days. The difference was, Billie worried about Giselle's physical health.

"Good for you." The older woman smiled with lips that drooped on one side as if she'd had a stroke. The doctors said the tests were inconclusive. Giselle said what did it matter under the circumstances. She was normally right.

"I can't wait to see them." Billie walked to her mother's side and placed her hand on her shoulder. "It will be painful in ways, I'll admit that." Tears filled her eyes. Billie often cried when she didn't want or need to. It happened because of the depression. The therapist said she tried too hard to be strong, and now she paid the price. But she had to try for herself and her mother. She had to be strong. She hoped the tears would stop someday.

Since the night she woke up trapped in the car with hardly a scratch, next to two bodies that had once been her husband and son, she suffered from PTSD. Post-Traumatic Stress Disorder—nothing to be trifled with— would take some time to get over. Her family could not come back. She had only her mother and her music to give her a reason to get out of bed in the morning. Survivor guilt was real.

Chapter 2

The Hurricane Hunters from the 53rd Weather Reconnaissance Squadron out of Keesler Air Force Base in Biloxi, Mississippi were on standby alert. Sandy had plans for the weekend, and now she had to cancel them. She knew the kids would understand, but they were tired of her always leaving just as the weather became warm. With spring break right around the corner, she wanted to take them home for a visit with their grandmother.

At least she didn't have to fly to the Hawaiian Islands this time. This time she could pack them off to Dad, who worked as many hours as she did, for a short period. She always downplayed the danger by saying "just another trip to the Atlantic" (or Pacific) depending upon where bad weather popped up this time. Her family didn't need to worry.

She was a proud part of the crew of the Lockheed WC-130J Hercules which flew directly into the hurricanes, sending back detailed information about the anomaly and gathering data on how the storm would track. The squadrons had been flying missions like this since 1946, and everything would be okay—she hoped. But as a scientist she couldn't show fear, especially in front of the kids. That would be all it took for her ex to have her back in court again as soon as she landed on dry land.

The first time she'd flown into the eye of the monster, she felt terrified and exhilarated at the same time. She loved her job and she hoped to instill in her kids the feelings of a job well done—a job you could really love—especially in her daughter. Carol, squeamish and clingy, unlike her "tom-boy" mother at her age, was a product of divorce. Major Sandra Miller's mother stayed at home as well as her dad on many days. His job in the auto maintenance shop he owned in town allowed him to devote his time to his family first. Many times, with nice weather, he would just close the doors and let the customers wait while he announced they were going on a picnic. Sandy and her sister were always happy to go play in the surf and watch Dad fish. As a child, Sandy lived the life of a beach bum. When she joined the Air Force, she soon encountered culture shock. The rest of the world did not have a beach in their back yard.

But weather had always been Sandy's first love. As a child, she would lay on the roof she accessed by climbing out her bedroom window and stare up at the puffy white clouds as they rolled overhead. Sometimes they weren't white and fluffy, though. Sometimes they were black and angry, and then she loved them even more. They were like friendly ghosts one day and deadly monsters the next. Maybe that was why she loved them so much—they were like her.

Her name had not been lost on her crew members who now called her "Hurricane Sandy" after the deadly nor'easter that hit New York and the eastern seashore. Her data was always accurate and right on point like the hurricane they named her after. In her element in a hurricane, she didn't know how she would live without the excitement someday when forced into retirement. But that worry was for another day. Today, she would gather information about the beautiful monster forming in the Gulf of Mexico.

"Mom, I can't find my blue shorts!" Sandy's daughter, Carol, could never find anything. It might be in her hand, but she was blind to the world sometimes.

Sandy walked into the girl's room which looked like the hurricane had already been through. Her suitcase lay on the unmade bed and shoes were strewn around the room. The closet door stood open, as well as every drawer of the dresser.

"I can't imagine why." Sandy walked to the bed and began looking through what the small weekend bag contained. "You mean these blue shorts? The ones I folded when I did laundry, and you put in your suitcase?"

Carol looked sheepish. "I guess I didn't see them."

"I guess not. Got your toothbrush? PJs? Got a jacket in case it gets cool?"

"Dad has toothbrushes, and I think I left my jacket there last time."

"Probably. Hustle, we leave in five minutes." Sandy smoothed her daughter's hair back from her face. She could be her twin, they looked so much alike, with honey-colored skin and blonde hair that hung straight as a string, unless tied back out of the way. Jake, on the other hand, favored his dad. Same red hair, and his freckled skin did not like the sun the way Carol's did. Sandy constantly chased him with sunscreen.

The children were less than a year apart in age but miles apart in personalities and looks. A lot like their parents. John Miller, a contractor to the Air Force,

12

worked in the finance department. The courtship between him and Sandy, like the marriage, was a whirlwind—and then the first child appeared. By the time the second came along, Sandy knew the relationship was on rocky ground. He traveled a lot for work, as did she, but with two babies at home, and a nanny doing most of the child care, John decided one day his wife needed to resign her commission and be a stay-at-home mom. He and the children needed her there. Well, the children did anyway. In the middle of the argument about Sandy's career choices, he took a long temporary duty out of state. She talked to him often on the phone, but one night when she called him after being up with a sick child, someone else answered the phone in a sleepy voice. Evidently, he didn't need her as much as he said he did.

"Okay, in the car in five minutes!" Sandy called down the hall toward her son's room. She knew he not only packed but probably inventoried the contents of his suitcase. His head emerged from the door of his room with ear buds plugged in and pulling the suitcase. He headed for the front door, hassling his sister along the way about not being ready to go.

"I'll be there in a minute!" Carol shouted at her brother, and Sandy knew she needed to head off another argument. Carol sat on the bed with tears running down her cheeks and her suitcase still not fully packed. Sandy held back the sigh she knew would only make things worse and walked back into her daughter's room again.

"Okay, let's see." She rummaged through the suitcase checking to make sure there were enough clothes. Three pair of shorts and three T-shirts. Shoes, pajamas and Mr. Elephant in the bottom. Carol hid him these days and only took him out to sleep with because of her brother's merciless teasing, but he was her security blanket with Mom gone.

"Sweetie, it looks like you need some panties." Sandy moved to the drawers and closed them one by one pulling out underwear to place in the suitcase.

"Mom, I hate it when you leave. I think you aren't coming back." Carol wiped her eyes with her palms.

"I always come back, honey. You know that. I have a job that requires me to travel sometimes. Someone has to keep us safe from storms, and the more we know about them, the safer we are."

"Well I wish someone else would do it instead of you." She looked up at her mother with green cat-like eyes.

Sandy hugged her daughter and looked at her tear stained eyes, then patted her on the back. "When I get back we'll get ready for Spring Break, okay? We're going to Grandma's for a whole week, and we can play in the sand and see Billie and have fun in the ocean. We'll be on vacation, okay?" Sandy zipped the suitcase closed and pulled it off the bed, handing it to her daughter. She could carry her own case. She needed to learn responsibility, but she also needed more mothering than her brother.

"Okay. I love to go to Grandma's and I want to look for starfish again."

"Starfish it is." Sandy put her hand on her daughter's shoulder and guided her out the door to the car and her waiting brother.

Chapter 3

The businesses in the harbor multiplied after the newly built marina. Slips for boats were often rented permanently. Snow birds from up north came down for the winter months to escape the cold. Also called Winter Texans, they lived in the Gulf of Mexico on boats they purchased and learned to pilot, some more adeptly than others. The harbor was cleaned and restored following a major hurricane. After the rebuilding, it became obvious the tourist trade could be prolonged past summer.

Neil Towers came down from Montana for the winter. Or maybe forever. After the divorce lawyers were finished with him, he lost all reason to go back home. She took the house and most everything else he owned and left him with the bills. He thought her his one true love, but she needed him to be there for her one hundred percent of the time and that didn't work for him. He thought he didn't need her, until she told him to leave, and then he found out just how empty life could be. He could have fought harder over the split, but why? The one thing of value he still owned was the convertible, his father's Mercedes coupe that he inherited from the estate. He packed up the car with the few things that would fit, placed the rest in storage, and drove south.

Drawn to the water like his dad, Neil's best

memories were the fishing trips they'd shared, and in the Gulf, he could fish every day. Catching something was great, but not necessary. Just sitting on the boat or the beach with a hat on his head and a line in the water was more relaxing than any spa. The fishing pole helped him feel the soul of the water—its back and forth motion had a reason, and it might be to relax the mind.

The boat rocked lazily in the afternoon light. Sun sparkled off dark green waves, and Neil's hat over his sunglasses covered any evidence that he dozed. Water droplets like diamonds ran down the line and into the larger body of water. The lazy quiet afternoon, only disturbed by an occasional screeching sea gull, came to life when the line jerked and tightened, spinning the reel. Neal, instantly awake, took his feet off the side of the boat and onto the deck; he pushed his hat back on his head and looked out in the water. Slowly winding the fishing line back into the reel, he tugged the pole up now and then. He had no idea what he'd hooked on the other end, but it felt desperate. He might have fish for dinner.

The silver-gray fish scales sparkled in the water as he pulled it in. Neil leaned over the side of the boat and pulled the fish in by the lip, so the hook would not pull through. The fish struggled, eyes bulging, tail flipping, out of his element. One minute the flounder was gliding along the bottom on its side—a bottom feeder it looked like one-half of a fish when brought on board the boat—the next minute it would be the perfect size fillet for one, paired with an ice-cold beer. Neil smiled. He had been living on canned food to keep from dining alone in a restaurant. Tonight, he would grill the wonderful fresh fish the sea gifted him.

Down the dock sat an old man in the shade of a building. He perpetually had a fishing pole in hand whenever Neil looked up. Neil had said hello to him a few times, and the man acted friendly but had little to say. Today as always, he sat with a line in the water and the man who owned the shrimper walked past him—stopped to talk a moment—and then gave him a bag of something. Maybe shrimp? Then the shrimper walked toward Neil.

"That's a good-looking flounder!" The man walked down the dock toward Neil. He smiled when he spoke, and Neil smiled back. "They go great with a cold beer."

"That is exactly what I thought. I'm Neil Towers by the way."

"Paul Smith, and that's my shrimper over there." He gestured to the large boat on the other side of the cove.

"Yes, I saw you come in. Did you catch many?" Neil pushed his hat back off his sweaty brow.

"We caught as many as always. You like shrimp?"

"Love 'em. Do you sell to customers right off the boat? I saw you give some to the old fisherman as you walked by. I guess that's what you gave him."

"You mean Poppy? He's a good guy, and I let him have some from time to time. But I'll sell to anyone. Most of my catch goes to Le Chez in town. Have you eaten there?" The shrimper's face was lined and leathery from years in the sun; he took off his sunglasses and revealed kind gray eyes.

"No, but I need to. I came down from Montana for the winter and haven't checked out the restaurants in town. I hate to eat alone in a room full of people.

Mostly I just eat here on my boat."

"Snow Bird, huh? Well, it's great to have you here. You Winter Texans help keep the economy going for us locals. I'll tell you, though, the chef at Le Chez is great, mostly because he has access to locally grown and harvested ingredients like my shrimp. And there is a lady here on the island who grows a wonderful vegetable garden that supplies a lot of the produce. They also have a new singer in the restaurant on the weekends. Well, she's not new; she used to live in Corpus Christi, but she is from the island originally and came back home. You should check Billie out, she's a jewel and has a set of lungs on her that would make Billie Holiday blush if she were still alive. But I'm taking up your time that you need to clean that fish. Enjoy your dinner and come get some shrimp sometime." Paul waved as he walked away.

"Will do," Neil said to the man's back.

Sea gulls swarmed overhead, smelling the blood spilled from the flounder as Neil cleaned it. He tossed the scraps overboard and the birds dove for them fighting for morsels. He then rinsed the blood from the back of the boat where he cleaned it. Taking the fillet into the kitchen, he refrigerated it until time to cook.

The boat, purchased not long after he arrived on the Gulf, became his new home. Before he took it out for a spin, he talked to the old timers around Sandhill Island, and they had told him about the new marina. That was his destination, at least for now. His brain formed a plan for a trip around the Gulf someday, maybe, but so far that thought stayed in the planning stages, just off the horizon.

The few things he bought at the local grocery store

included potatoes, and he would cut one up to cook with the fish tonight. He needed to go in to the grocery store again soon. Maybe tomorrow night he might try out the restaurant. It had been a long time since he heard a talented jazz singer and wondered if an island so small could accommodate the talent Paul talked about.

Chapter 4

Billie padded into her mother's bedroom barefoot in a short spaghetti-strapped dress made of gold lame´. It had a long sheer jacket that flowed in the wind when she moved her arms. The sheer jacket worked as a good stage prop as it reflected light from the setting sun and waved in the ocean breeze. She owned a few cocktail dresses that she wore when she performed and tried to change them up a little now and then. Since she only sang three nights a week, it wasn't too hard.

"You look just like a golden sunset." Giselle smiled her droopy smile at her daughter with high heels in one hand and flip flops in the other. Billie would walk in flip flops the couple of blocks to the restaurant and then put on the shoes that went with the dress.

"Well, thank you. I hope the voice is as golden."

"You know it will be," her mother replied.

Billie kissed her mother goodbye and walked out the door sliding into the flip flops as she went. Raven would stay until Billie returned so Giselle would not be alone.

Billie sang on Friday, Saturday, and Sunday nights at Le Chez. The chef offered her the job as soon as he found out she came home. There weren't a lot of places to work on the island, and Billie didn't want a full-time job just yet. She still had a lot of healing to do. A part-time job was better than no job on Sandhill Island.

Giselle's house, paid for long ago, and Billie's expenses small, they could live there for a long time. Billie's psychiatric bills were paid by the Texas Victims Compensation Fund, and her mother had Medicare for her healthcare needs. The two women lived simply and took care of each other.

When she pulled open the back door to the restaurant, the smell of spices and fish overwhelmed her. Sam's little restaurant on the tiny tourist island was one of the best kept secrets in Texas. She walked past the planned chaos of the kitchen and through to the deck that sat off the side of the building. The chef added it to take care of the overflow of customers in the small building. Many people liked to eat outdoors when the weather allowed. Then he had a stage built off one end of the deck near the tables and chairs. With good weather, the deck opened, and the diners were treated to dinner and a show.

"Hey, pretty lady." A tall dark-skinned man in a Hawaiian shirt smiled at her from the stage. He tuned his string bass that sat next to the piano. His leathery skin wrinkled when he smiled, and his almost black eyes twinkled. Alfred Stringer, aka String, performed as her bass accompaniment. She played piano and sang most tunes, but he could take over and tickle the ivories better than she could and did on occasion. He could also sing vocals as melodious as his stringed instrument. String, a legend in the Corpus Christi jazz world, came to the island because of Billie and soon made it his home too. Not only her bass player, he was also her mentor and friend. He stayed with her in the hospital after her family died, and through the trial that followed. He cared for her like the brother she never had. She knew he got offers all the time to come back to Corpus Christi for a lot more money than he made at Le Chez, but he wouldn't leave her.

His mother had pressed him to live the life of a musician—not a teacher. He had the talent to make a living doing what he loved and not be tied to the constraints of a school board and the lessons they forced her to teach. He was a free spirit unlike her, and she wanted to watch him soar.

Mom called him Ally or Alfred when in trouble. String came later in the smoky bars on dimly lit stages playing music to often-times rude and drunk crowds. But he became quickly known in Corpus Christi circles as the bass fiddle player everyone wanted to play with. He soon would make a living doing what he loved. Mom was right.

Before he even graduated from high school, Alfred played in the Corpus Christi jazz district on the weekends late at night. Not yet of legal age, he was often paid under the table after being let in the back door secretly. At least he got paid. There were times when some bands could have cheated him out of a paycheck—and tried—but his music kept the crowds coming in; management didn't want to lose the bass fiddle player known as String.

Then one night he met her. The dark-haired woman in the gold dress walked in looking out of place, nervous. Her first time at that bar. No one in the band knew her, but somehow, she managed to get an audition. She walked to the microphone, adjusting it to her height like she put off the inevitable, and opened her mouth.

It was love at first sight. Not romantic love, more

like a little sister, but it was love, and String would do anything to protect his sister. Billie Stone had the voice of an angel. She crooned into the microphone, and the crowd stood still. She didn't just sing into the microphone; she made love to the microphone. No, she became the music, and it flowed in and out of her like the instrument she was. String had a sister for the first time in his life and he would be by her side always.

They became famous together in the Corpus Christi jazz scene playing and singing together. His strings, whether bass or guitar, melded with her voice as one.

"String, how's it going? Ready for the rowdy shrimp eaters tonight?" Billie adjusted the height on the mic stand and ran her hands over the keys of the piano. How it stayed in tune being moved back and forth from inside to outside with changes in humidity and temperature remained a miracle to her.

"Oh, I can handle some shrimp eaters, as long as they don't throw those tails at us."

"Just keep on playing if they do." She smiled back at his teasing. "How about a little Joplin tonight? You up for it?"

"Always up for Janis." String ran his fingers over the frets of the bass and picked the tune like he had played it all his life. Maybe he had.

Waiting until a few diners were seated outside at the tables with hurricane lamps in the middle, the duet began, slowly at first with some of the quieter tunes and then branched out. Everyone knew Janis Joplin's music, and a certain set was expected of a jazz singer.

A man Billie had not seen before sat up front. Snow Bird, she thought. They spent their money just like everyone else and without them, there would be little to do in the winter on the island. His pink skin—not used to the semi-tropical sun of the south Texas coast—said he was not from around here. He looked awkward by himself and drank domestic beer with his meal. However, he was no stranger to shrimp.

He smiled at her, and she looked away. She did not need a tourist hitting on her. Not that it didn't happen, but she was not interested. Even with his sweet boyish grin.

She took a drink from the bottled water Sam left for her on the piano and went into another tune when she saw Sandy's Uncle Paul walk out onto the deck. Sandy's uncle had never met a stranger, and he walked up to the Snow Bird's table shaking his hand. Of course, Paul knew everyone.

"You decided to come out." Paul sat at the table as if offered a seat. "She's great, isn't she?"

Billie could over-hear part of the conversation as they took a break. She swallowed the water again letting it roll down her over-worked throat.

"Yes, she is. No offense, but why is she here and not on a bigger stage in a larger community?"

"She's home." Paul gestured to the island.

"That I understand. This place is wonderful. No traffic and light breezes."

"Until you live through one of our hurricanes," Paul laughed. "Then you might prefer traffic on a crowded freeway. But you can experience that too on your way off the island to safer ground."

"Every place has its problems. But do you know the jazz singer? Can you introduce her to me?" Neil fingered the label on the beer bottle.

"I can, but she's not interested, man. She is a

widow and lost her family in a car accident. Let's just say she's fragile."

"I'm not looking for a date. Just got over a bad break-up too. I just wanted to tell her how much I enjoyed the show."

"There's a tip jar." Paul looked at Neil knowingly.

"Right. Okay. Thanks for the info, and I'll be by to get some of that shrimp from you one of these days. I might not be able to make it taste as good as this tonight though."

"Anytime. See you around." Paul walked back to his table where his wife waited.

Chapter 5

As a used car salesman, Joe Franks once worked at a lucrative dealership. He once owned a house—nothing fancy but a roof over his head. Now he rented a one-bedroom apartment in Corpus Christi and delivered pizzas. Everything he ever owned taken from him, all because of some confusion one night on the road.

He hadn't had that much to drink. He and his buddies played cards every Friday after work, and they had beer, but not that much. In a night so dark he got confused going home a different way, suddenly the minivan appeared in front of him. He swerved, too late. He didn't intend to kill anyone. He never hurt a fly until that night, but the way the woman carried on you would have thought he was a serial killer. If she had died too, it might have been easier for him. As it turned out, he spent a year in jail on an involuntary manslaughter charge and lost everything he ever owned. She had issues, the courts said, and he had to pay her doctor bills. Well, after a year in jail, he had issues too. Issues like no one wanted to hire him anymore.

The aging Buick bucked one last time as he pulled into the parking lot of the run-down apartment building. It needed a tune-up and maybe some new belts and hoses. It had a lot of miles on it when he bought it, and now even more.

"That'll be eighteen ninety-five with tax." Joe

looked at the young man with tattoos standing in the doorway. The smell of weed wafted through the open door. The young man sneered.

"Hey boys, the pizza dude wants eighteen ninety-five. Anybody got any money?" Laughter came from inside the room. He'd already pulled the pizza from the insulated holder. The man with the tattoos held one end in his hands. "Better come inside, pizza dude, if you want to get paid."

Franks knew better than to walk into the room, but he needed the money. He stepped into the doorway holding one end of the pizza box like it would save his life. There were three hoods standing inside, each one bigger than the last, and a woman lay on the bed watching TV, looking bored. No one had their wallet out.

He looked around the room. "Eighteen ninety-five." Maybe they needed confirmation as to the price.

Something hard jammed into his ribs from behind. Franks gasped. "I hope you got more than eighteen ninety-five, pizza dude. I hope you have a lot more." He could smell the sour breath of old whisky behind him that he knew belonged to the man with the gun in his ribs.

"I don't have any money, guys. This is the first delivery of the evening. The only thing I have is some change." He lied. He always had money in the glove box of the car, but they didn't need to know that.

A hand reached in to his pocket pulling the few bills and some change and turned it inside out. Then the second pocket, empty except for keys. Joe felt the wallet pulled from his back pocket, with only a driver's license and debit card. They could have the debit card—it was attached to a near-empty bank account anyway.

"That's it?" The gunman shoved the barrel further into his ribs.

"I told you, I just got started tonight." Franks knew there were other deliveries in the back seat and they might be just what saved his life tonight. Maybe they'd believe him.

The woman looked up and pulled a string of bubble gum from her mouth twirling it on the end of a chipped and ragged nail.

"I'm hungry man. Let's see how many pizzas he got with him." One hood from the other side of the room grabbed the keys from the hand of the first and walked out to the car. The door creaked as it opened, and the hungry man climbed inside. He let out a satisfied yelp, then backed out with a tower of pizzas wrapped in insulated bags. "We hit the mother-load, boys!"

Franks stood still, wondering what the next move might be. He didn't need the bags back even though he knew they'd be taken out of the next pay check, along with the price of the pizzas.

"Go back and look in the glove box, idiot. He's probably got money in there." Franks stiffened involuntarily, trying not to show his hand. But the man with the gun was intent on the hood with the pizzas and didn't notice.

The man tossed the pizzas on the table with a huff and walked back out to the car pulling the door open. The glove box held maps and receipts from repairs. The money, well hidden in a compartment most people didn't know existed, stayed hidden. Joe found it accidently one day feeling deep inside the compartment when the flashlight he needed slid behind.

"Empty, boss." The hungry robber walked back in the door heading straight for the table full of pizza that the others were already devouring.

"Well, it must be your lucky day, pizza dude." The man with the gun dangled the keys in front of his face then threw them out the door and shoved him after them. One last kick in the pants, and the door slammed behind him. The keys twinkled in the street light.

Franks ran for the parking lot, grabbed the keys off the ground as he yanked open the car door. He jumped into the car, shaking as he turned the key. The car grunted on the first try—and then the engine caught. He left rubber as he raced out of the parking lot, happy to be alive.

The explanation at the pizza restaurant was not enough. Franks knew it wouldn't be. He would have to pay for the pizzas he lost as well as the bags out of his own check. But he was done for the evening. Nothing would put him back out on the street tonight, no matter what the boss said.

Unlocking the door to his shabby apartment with a newspaper tucked in the crook of his arm, he found a letter under his door. Slitting the envelope open, he dropped it on the floor as he shut the door behind him. Due to inflation and the high cost of everything, rent just went up another hundred dollars—and it was a week until the first of the month. He wadded the note and threw it across the room then reached in the refrigerator for a beer. Something he couldn't have these days, but who would tell his parole officer? He plopped into the worn-out recliner and opened the paper. He no longer shook like a school girl over the incident—a year in the joint and he had seen everything—but one thing was certain, he had to find a different way to make a living.

An article on the entertainment page caught his attention. Billie Stone, a jazz singer—a popular one. But after the accident, she disappeared. She no longer sang the blues—or at least not in Corpus Christi—according to the paper. She went home. He had no idea where.

He was sorry for her misfortune, and for his own. He'd paid enough. They called it an accident, and if he could take it back, he would. His old boss at least financed a car for him when he got out so he could work, but would not hire him back. The car dealership had a reputation to uphold, they said, and they couldn't have jail birds running around the office.

Maybe he should try to find her—check out where she used to work to see if anyone knew where she went. Maybe if he talked to her she might write him a letter of recommendation or something. He needed a better job, and he had paid his debt to society. Surely, she would see things his way.

He'd try the jazz section of town to find out if anyone knew where she went.

****

After deliveries the next night, he stepped into the dark and smoky jazz club. He almost choked on the smell of stale beer and cigarettes. His eyes adjusted to the lights, and he walked to the bar. He had enough in tips to at least buy a beer—even if he didn't drink it. He didn't need alcohol on his breath while driving, but he knew a bartender would never talk to him if he didn't buy something. And bartenders knew everything.

"Whatever you have on tap," he said hoping the bartender didn't have much to choose from. He plunked some cash down on the bar and turned around to look at the band. They played loudly, but not well. At least not what he wanted to hear.

The bartender placed the glass in front of him and gathered up the cash.

"Thanks, man," Franks said. "By the way, Billie Stone still singing here?"

The bartender shook his head. "She hasn't been here for a couple of years," and he began to walk away.

"Know where I might find her?" Franks picked up the beer and lifted it to his lips. The hoppy scent crawled up his nose, but he didn't take a sip. He couldn't afford to. Prison was behind him, he wasn't going back.

"Murphy might know." He pointed to the stage. "He's the bass player."

"Thanks man." As if on cue the band ended the set and began to pick up their instruments. Late, even for a bar. Night had to end sometime.

Franks walked toward the stage, beer in hand, dodging tables and customers who stood to leave. The stage sat up one step at the front of the room. Amps unplugged and cords stowed, the bass player reached around the equipment picking up his guitar case.

"You Murphy?" Franks stepped up on the small stage.

"Who wants to know?" asked the man with the greasy hair.

"Me." Franks smiled. "I'm looking for Billie Stone and the bartender said you might know where to find her."

"Billie left town. And who did you say you were?"

"Just a friend. Well, more of a fan. I used to listen to her. Man, that woman has a set of pipes!"

"Yeah, she does. But I don't know where she is. You might try some other places down the street. She sang in all of them." He clicked the guitar case closed and stood.

Franks walked back toward the front door placing the untouched beer on the bar as he left. He'd try another night, another bar.

Chapter 6

The weather during spring break could mean anything. The college kids would be out in full force no matter the conditions. Being seen on the beach during spring break was the important thing, even if you had goose bumps. Sandy and her kids weren't college kids.

Sandy made sure her kids had swimsuits, shorts, jeans and jackets. She might have a hard time getting them into them, but at least they would have what they needed. Shoes were another story. She knew about being a barefoot kid growing up on a beach and found flight boots confining, but the Air Force said she had to wear them. She understood the mindset of the kids even if she had to be a responsible mom.

She drove the loaded minivan to the dock where the ferry went across to the island. Carol loved this part of the journey to Grandma's. Sometimes they saw dolphins alongside chasing the ferry in its endless journeys back and forth.

"I can't wait to see Grandma!" Her straight blonde hair flew in the breeze of the open windows as they waited in line for the ferry's return.

"You're such a dork." Her brother, with his eyes always on the video game in his hand, still had an ear pointed toward things around him. Good for him. And he never missed an opportunity to hassle his sister. Not so good.

"Jake, what did we say about picking on your sister?" Sandy hated arguing with her kids on vacation. But the bullying had to stop, and eventually it would be Carol who had to stop it.

"*You* said not to."

"That's right. I said not to. So, why are you?" Sandy looked in the rear-view mirror to see Carol sticking her tongue out at her brother. "And Carol, knock it off. We are here to have fun, not fight. Grandma won't put up with it. She'll have you both doing chores."

"I don't know why we always have to go to Grandma's." A year older than Carol, Jake, almost in his teens, didn't want to be seen with his little sister or grandmother. Tweens they called them. Children were becoming more and more sophisticated these days. Or they thought they were. They read the articles and knew how they were supposed to act at a certain age. Or how the manuals said they were supposed to act. Sandy disagreed.

"Because she's your grandmother and she has an ocean in her back yard. How many kids can say that?" She wouldn't show up at her mother's house arguing with her son.

"Most of the kids that live in Biloxi or up and down the Gulf Coast." Jake's eyes never left the electronic device in his hands.

"All right, enough. Here comes the ferry. You don't open the doors until I tell you that you can. Everybody got that?" Sandy knew they loved to stand by the railing and watch the trip over to the island. A murmur from the back seat said they understood.

The car parked and the kids at the railing watching

the water for signs of dolphins, Sandy breathed deeply leaning against the van. Jake was right about one thing. They did live near the ocean, but Biloxi was not like Sandhill Island. Island life felt slower, and the beach was just blocks away. The island even smelled different than the city. She knew that keeping the kids within eye-sight would be tough the older they got. The pull of the water just too great.

Back in the car, they drove off the ferry onto the island and then turned left toward her mother's home. Like most houses on the island, a small bungalow. Not much to look at, but it was home. She drove past the market area and saw the restaurant where Billie sang. She would take the kids and Mom to see her—maybe tonight. Billie only worked on the weekends. She drove past the blank space in the downtown area that once held a vegetable stand that blew down in a hurricane. Meg no longer sat there selling her vegetables. The rumor that Meg only sold to Le Chez and the grocery store in town now could be true. She was never seen sitting in the heat waiting for customers to come to her. Meg's little beach house blew away in the hurricane, and she rebuilt in the same spot, a much bigger and nicer home. But she still had her garden.

Past the few bars on the island and into the small neighborhood where Billie spent her childhood, sat her mother's home. It needed a good coat of paint. Maybe Sandy could hire a contractor while here and get that taken care of. She'd have to do it on the sly, because Mom would never allow it. But if she paid him in advance, what could Mom do? It had been yellow with white shutters. Sandy wondered what color her mother preferred.

"Grandma!" Sandy barely stopped the car before Carol was out the door running for the front porch.

Jake sighed, but for once had no comment. He climbed out of the car slowly, plugged into his phone, and slammed the door. Sandy knew from experience he would not like the wrath of Grandma if he kept up that attitude.

Martha stood from the rocking chair placing her crochet project in the basket at her feet next to the glass of ice tea. She smiled and walked to the aging steps of the porch with her arms outstretched, enfolding her granddaughter in an embrace.

"How's my favorite granddaughter?" She hugged her again.

"Fine." Carol smiled up her, and Sandy realized how much her daughter was beginning to look like her.

"And my favorite grandson?" She tugged Jake's sleeve as he attempted to walk past her into the house. She pulled him into a quick hug.

"Hi Grandma," he said continuing to look bored with the adults.

Martha nodded at Jake then looked at Sandy.

"Hi, Mom." Sandy hugged her mom and rolled her eyes toward Jake. They both knew what it meant. Just ignore him, he'll come around.

"I have a pitcher of tea on the table and some fresh baked cookies. Does anyone want cookies?" Cookies got Jake's attention, and he looked up.

"We'd love some." Sandy hugged her again. "And then we'll unload the car. I want to take us all to Le Chez for dinner tonight." Sandy licked the sugar off her fingers from the cookie she ate. Her mother's sugar cookie was the best she had ever eaten. Sandy tried to duplicate the recipe but never with the same success as her mother.

"Oh, that is so expensive! Let's just eat here." Martha smiled at her grandchildren quietly eating cookies.

"Billie is singing tonight, and I want to hear her. She only sings on the weekends. If we go early, we can sit on the deck and listen to our favorite jazz singer, and Jake might get enough shrimp to fill him up."

"I can eat a bunch," he said around the sugar cookie and smiled. At least he still smiled about food.

"Okay, we'll eat in tomorrow night then." Martha refilled Sandy's glass with tea.

Sandy knew her mother didn't have a lot of money but was comfortable. However, when three more people invaded her house, it could cause a strain on the food budget. Especially when one tween had the appetite of a professional football player.

Chapter 7

The four of them walked the few blocks on dirt roads to the small restaurant, and Sandy opened the door to Le Chez. The smell of garlic bread and shrimp scampi hit her. Did they have garlic in heaven? Sam, the owner and chef, stood in the door to the kitchen fanning himself. When he saw Sandy, he broke into a grin she could see across the darkened room. He walked quickly to her with his hands out.

"Hurricane Sandy!" He was the only one besides her crew members who ever called her that. He hugged her warmly and then Carol and Martha. Jake stuck out his hand quickly for Sam to shake. She'd made him leave the electronics at home. The boy was smart and could be sociable if he needed to. "And Master Jake." Sam beamed. "So good to see all of you. Carol, you are getting prettier every day, and Martha, we don't see much of you anymore."

"Well, we're here for the week, and we wanted to pay you, and the local talent, a visit." Sandy touched the top of her daughter's head, smoothing her hair back out of her face.

"If you're on the island for a week, you'd better be in my restaurant several times then." Sam hugged Sandy again. "So beautiful," he said, holding her at arms-length. "Come, I've saved you a table up front near the jazz singer. She has already started, but I know

38

she can't wait to see you."

Billie was belting out a Billie Holiday song when they walked out onto the deck. She saw her friend and waved as they were seated up front near the stage. She finished her song and spoke into the mic.

"My good friend Major Sandra Miller and family!" Billie, gesturing to the table where Sandy and family were sitting, then broke into her rendition of Billie Holiday's famous *God Bless the Child.*

"She's good, Mom." Carol looked with adoring eyes at her mother's friend decked out in a shimmery aqua gown looking like a mermaid.

"How come she sings here, Mom? Why not in Corpus Christi or something. She really is good." Jake agreed with something his sister said and could make intelligent conversations without the constant electronics. She needed to put a limit on them. In a busy family, distractions were often ignored.

"She used to, but now she's home again." Sandy felt unsure how much information to give her kids about Billie.

"Well, she needs to go back." Jake said, playing with his napkin. "I mean this seems like a waste. She could be on Broadway."

Sandy looked at her son, so pragmatic, like his father

"Why doesn't she go back, Mom?" Carol looked again with adoring eyes at her mother's friend on the stage.

"She lost her family in a car accident," Sandy began, and her mother interrupted.

"And her mother is sick, so she is looking after her too."

"Well, if I could sing like that, I'd go to Broadway and not stay home to look after my mom!" Jake shrugged and dropped the napkin back in its place.

"Jake! I'm surprised at you. Your mother works very hard for you and if she needed you, I would think you'd be there to help her, too." Martha looked sternly at her only grandson.

"I'm sorry, Grandma. I just thought maybe someone else could look after her mom, is all."

The waiter appeared as if by magic and handed around the menus and a basket of homemade yeast rolls. Jake ordered the all-you-could-eat shrimp.

After dinner Billie still sang. Sandy, stuffed with seafood, raptly listening to her friend, and wondering where she got that talent, realized she was unaware of those around her. Her mother placed a hand on her arm and nodded at Carol dozing off at the table. Jake fidgeted after eating an entire ocean of shrimp, and Sandy knew she needed to take the kids home.

"I'll take them home. You stay until she's finished. You two need to catch up." Martha stood and jostled Carol. "Come on sweetie, let's go home."

"Is she finished?" Carol rubbed her eyes and looked up.

"Not yet, but soon. Come on we'll walk home." Martha took her granddaughter's arm, and Sandy knew she had kept the kids out too late.

"I'll be home soon, Mom." She kissed her daughter and patted her son on the shoulder as they walked out through the restaurant.

The last song sung, Sandy moved to the stage to help Billie put things away. Sam appeared as if by magic waking the drunk in the back and escorting him out the door. He then stepped up on the small stage.

"My two favorite women." He smiled. "Have a drink with me?"

"You know I can't have anything, Sam. But Sandy might." Billie raised her eyebrows at her friend asking.

"Maybe one, if we all sit down together." Sandy knew Billie could not drink with her meds.

Sam miraculously produced a bottle of chardonnay and two wine glasses. He nodded at a waiter for a glass of tea for Billie.

Sandy sat down and kicked off her shoes, leaning back in her chair. The waves rolled in and the light breeze blew through her hair. She leaned forward, took a sip and looked at her best friend from school.

"How are you? You look and sound great! Are you really as good as you seem?" Sandy eyed her friend looking for a sign she was as relaxed as she appeared.

"Maybe. I think so, and then sometimes I'm not so sure. But your kids…" She shook her head and tried not to cry. "They are so wonderful!"

"Well, sometimes they are!" Sandy brushed the hair out of her face. "They're great. I love them. But like I said, sometimes…"

Both women giggled as Sam sat down between them. "What's so funny?" he asked turning the chair around and sitting with it between his legs.

"Kids. They can be a handful." Sandy took another sip.

"Well, you've got a couple of keepers," Sam said.

"I know I do. And how are the two of you? Still keeping the island going, I see." Sandy sipped again.

"Sure." Sam wiped the sweat from his brow. "Still chasing clouds?"

"Oh, you know it." The three old friends talked into the night, and then Sandy found Billie leaning on her elbow like her daughter. She seemed to be wearing everyone out tonight. Swallowing the last of the wine, she stood and took her friend by the elbow. "You need to go home and so do I. I'll be here for the week and plan to see both of you a lot. Sam, thank you for the drink. So good to see you again." She kissed him on the top of his head and walked barefoot off the deck, shoes in hand, into the sand with Billie in tow.

In the distance, she could see a skinny dog hanging around out back of the restaurant. Sam probably fed a stray. How it got to the island, she couldn't even guess.

Strolling the direction they used to walk home from school, Sandy breathed deeply the island breeze. "I don't know why I ever left this place." But she knew why; there were very few careers on Sandhill Island and none for a meteorologist. She could see Billie's house in the distance and they walked into the yard. "I'll see you tomorrow." She hugged her friend and then walked away.

Chapter 8

The smell of coffee and maple syrup woke Billie from a deep sleep. Raven had cooked breakfast again. With the window open, she could hear the gulls cry and smell the ocean breeze. Pulling on her cotton robe, she walked into the kitchen where her mother sat in the wheel chair at the kitchen table happily talking to Raven.

"Your pancakes are wonderful even when you eat them with a spoon." The older woman stirred the concoction in the bowl in front of her. Raven poured milk and sugar into the coffee before placing it on the tray for Giselle, making sure the beverage wasn't too hot.

"Good morning ladies." Billie kissed her mother's cheek and poured herself a cup of coffee.

"And a good morning to you, Billie. I'll have some more pancakes ready in a minute and there's sausage on a plate by the stove." Raven stood near the stove with a spatula in hand.

"Thank you, Raven. You're a dear." Billie sipped the hot coffee needing to wake up a little before eating a full breakfast.

Raven sliced a banana and dropped it into the pancake batter poured onto the griddle. "Your mother woke up hungry this morning and said she wanted pancakes. I say, if the woman wants pancakes then she shall have them!" She smiled around a mouthful of pearly teeth.

"You're so sweet," Billie said to the nurse cooking breakfast. Where would you find someone else like her, she wondered, and hoped she never had to try. "Sandy and her family came to the restaurant last night, and we plan to go to the beach today. I'm sure they'll be by soon. I want to show them to you. The kids are so big."

"Oh, that's wonderful. I can't wait to see them." The older woman's hand shook as she lifted the spoon to her droopy mouth and managed to insert it on the second try.

"You need some help, Mom?" Billie wondered how long the woman would last and would she be able to stay in her home until the inevitable end. She shuddered involuntarily thinking of going through another funeral. But she knew it would happen someday. No one got out alive, her mother always said of death.

"No, dear, I'm fine. Eat your breakfast."

Billie wiped her mother's chin anyway. Just because she didn't want to be fed like a baby didn't mean she should sit with food on her face. Billie understood her mother would want to be clean.

A hot plate of pancakes and sausage materialized in front of Billie, and Raven turned back to the stove after the delivery.

"If you keep feeding me like this, all those sparkly gowns will have to be let out." Billie looked up at Raven, and then poured syrup across the mound of pancakes she knew she would not be able to finish. The phone in her robe pocket rang. The screen read Sandy.

"Hey Sandy, good morning. How are the

munchkins?" Billie put a bite of pancake in her mouth.

"Hungry. They are like baby birds with their mouths always open." The noise of children playing rang in the background.

"They're great. I loved seeing them last night." Billie sipped her coffee.

"Well, they can't wait to see 'Aunt Billie' this morning. Either that or they are anxious to get to the beach. You know we live in Biloxi and see the beach all the time, but I guess an island beach is different. Something about island life is not the same."

"Yeah, it is a lot more laid back, and that's good." Sandy shoved a fork in her mouth loaded with pancake and a piece of sausage she stabbed along the way.

"They want to know when we can come by and take you to the beach. I also want to say hi to your mom as well."

"Tell them I'm still in my pajamas and eating breakfast, but I could be done by the time you get here, that is if they don't run." It warmed Billie's heart to think of running and giggling children. She shoved a couple more mouthfuls of food in her mouth rinsing them down with juice and coffee, then stood taking her plate to the sink. "Ladies, I'm going to brush my teeth and put on a swimsuit. The noisy hordes are coming."

Before she got back from changing Billie heard voices and knocking on the front door.

"Kids, be quiet. Giselle isn't feeling well, and she doesn't need your noise." Sandy stood in front of the door with Jake and Carol jostling for position. "Go wait on the swing." She pointed to the porch swing with the floral cushion and afghan swaying in the breeze. They ran for the swing, Carol wrapping in the throw as if cold.

Billie opened the door and hugged her best friend in the world. "Hey, guys. So good to see you." She stood aside holding the door open as Raven pushed the wheel chair out onto the porch.

Immediately the noise and movement ceased.

"Sandy! Oh, and look how big your kids have gotten. Lordy." Giselle held out a frail hand, and Sandy took it, kissing it lightly.

"Giselle, you look lovely as usual. You remember Jake and Carol." They both stood from the porch swing, looking shy. They were tormenting each other a moment ago.

"Hi," they said in unison.

"Oh, it is so good to see you!" She smiled at the children and held out her arms for them to come to her. They walked over and accepted the gentle hug.

"Giselle, can you not walk anymore?" Carol, the baby, was the first to speak.

"Carol! That's not a nice question." Sandy looked embarrassed.

"No, it's fine," Giselle's crooked mouth attempted to smile. "No, honey, the old legs have finally given up. But I haven't. I'm still here. And you two have grown so much! Are you having fun at your grandmother's for spring break?"

They both nodded.

"It's a little boring. She doesn't even have Wi-Fi." Jake broke the silence.

"Well, who needs Wi-Fi when you have the ocean, huh?" Giselle folded her robe neatly over her gown and looked longingly out to sea. The ocean, only a block away, and the beach where they swam two blocks, but still visible from her front porch.

Billie reached back in the door and picked up a bag with her towel and sunscreen, plopped a hat on her head, sunglasses on her face, and announced she could be found on the beach if needed. She kissed her mother goodbye and signaled to Raven she had her phone. Just in case. She couldn't wait to get to the beach.

Without discussing it, the two women went to their regular spot. They walked to it as if by radar. An entire island surrounded by sand and they had one beach they wanted to use.

There he sat. A fisherman had their spot. He sat in the low-slung beach chair with a surf rod stuck in the sand. The hat on his head hid his face but his legs looked young.

"Kids, let's move down a little way. You don't want to get into his fishing line." Sandy called to the boy and girl who were already in the water, waving her hand and gesturing to move to the left.

"Who does he think he is taking our beach?" Billie giggled at her friend.

"I know, really. He has the whole ocean and he likes this spot. But it is a perfect place; it's hard to blame him."

The fisherman looked up and waved. Sandy waved back as Billie slightly lifted a hand. He was, after all, in her spot.

The women set down the bags and pulled towels from them spreading them on the sand. Neither brought a beach chair.

"You know, the older I get, the more I think I need a chair. Used to be I just plunked my young butt on the sand and never thought twice."

"But your butt and mine are about the same age, and I know what you mean. The sand never used to be this hard!" Billie sat on the towel shrugging off her cover-up and lathering on sunscreen. "I hate to act like a tourist, but I need to find those beach chairs in the utility room closet."

"I guess so. Not as comfortable as it used to be." Sandy dug her toes in the sand. "And I need a pedicure. Flight boots can do a number on your feet." She picked at the polish that remained on her big toe.

"Well, the sand is great for scrubbing, you know." Billie dug a hole in the sand, sticking her foot into it and then began to rub the course particles around her cuticles and heels.

"So, tell me. How are you really?" Sandy looked at Billie over the top of her sunglasses. "You look great. I have never heard you sing so beautifully, but are you really doing okay?"

"I guess as good as I can. I don't have the nightmares anymore. I do yoga each day and meditation."

"I saw the stones on the porch."

"Yes, I did that one day when it rained, and I couldn't go to the beach. Mom loves them, so I leave them there. It is all part of the meditation the doctor has me doing. I have to say, I thought it was a crock at first, but she's right. It helps." Both women looked up at squealing in the distance. The kids were splashing and giggling in hip deep water.

"I just hope he doesn't drown her," Sandy said, watching her children. "They fight all the time anymore. He is only a year older, but he is sure he's in charge, and she's just a baby sister in his way. He is so much like his dad, but she isn't really like me. I don't know who she's like."

"Carol is just herself, I guess." Billie watched the young blonde head go under the water and come up yards away from where she started. She held something dangling from her hand. Running toward the beach she shrieked. "I think she found a starfish."

"She's been talking about that since we left home. She said she wanted to go Grandma's and look for starfish. At least that's what she said after the crying fit about Mom leaving her all the time, and she thought Mom might not come back."

"Wow! That's new, isn't it? I mean you've always traveled, so why the change?"

"I've been wondering that myself." Sandy took the offered sunscreen and rubbed it on her shoulders. Carol dumped the starfish on her mother's towel, and then trotted back to the water. "And I've been thinking. The last trip was eventful. I mean we weren't in immediate danger…yes, we were. We almost ended up in the drink. We suffered a four-engine rollback in the eye of the storm. I'm the one who said we needed to get inside the eye of the hurricane for better data. Then after a lightning strike, we lost all four engines. The C-130 turned into a 50-ton glider that had to be mechanically maneuvered. Thankfully we had an excellent crew. We landed at Key West. Then we slid to the end of the runway, unable to use the auxiliary pump to slow us down, because the mechanic thought we might catch fire. The weather was turbulent and I was a hot mess when we finally landed. Thankfully we all survived, but the plane suffered substantial damage."

"Good grief, Sandy!" Billie looked horrified.

"I could think of nothing but my kids. I mean after what happened to you…" Sandy trailed off. "And I'm considering doing something different. I mean what if something happened to me? How would my kids handle it?"

"Well, we all know that it doesn't take a plane crash—just driving your car can be dangerous." Billie thought of the car crash again that left her without a family.

"I'm sorry. I shouldn't have brought it up." Sandy touched her arm.

"No, it has to be dealt with. I can't just push it down and try to imagine it never happened. It did. But if you're thinking about doing something else, that is a big deal. We should be able to discuss it. I can handle it."

"I know you can. And as far as my situation, I've been looking at options. I've been thinking of teaching. I don't know. You know meteorology is all I ever wanted to do. I used to love the excitement and danger. Maybe I'm getting old or something." The air was silent, and both women looked out to sea. Friends for a lifetime, they often did not need to talk to communicate. Billie knew her friend would make the right decision. She was an excellent mother and meteorologist.

Billie stood, took off her sunglasses and hat and tossed them onto the towel. "You are getting old," she said grinning, and ran for the water. Sandy trotted after her splashing into the surf near the kids, taking the starfish back to the relative safety of the ocean with her. Carol might find it again.

The noise caused the stray dog in the distance to

look up from its scrap. Kids were always fun to play with. But the dog stuck to the shadows—at least for now.

****

The last pizza delivered and the tip money stuffed in his pocket—the small one, it wasn't much money—Joe Franks drove his beat-up sedan to the jazz district again. The car would never be the same and would eternally smell like pizza. He didn't know how he would ever be able to sell it. But he didn't have the money to upgrade anyway. He just hoped it ran long enough for him to get a better job. He was a car salesman, not a delivery boy. There had to be a better way to make a living.

"She used to sing here man, but after the accident, she never came back. A cryin' shame. A voice like that… But I guess she just lost the urge to go on. Uh, um." The bartender polished the glass. "You gonna drink that beer or just look at it?"

"Do you know where she went?" Franks took a sip of the beer and tried not to like it too much.

"Home, I think. Her mom got sick, so they probably look after each other now."

"Where's home?" Franks sipped again.

"You with the police or somethin'?" The bartender reached for another spotless glass to polish.

"No, just knew her and wanted to touch base, you know." Franks sipped again.

"Well, you'll never get her back here, but I heard she grew up on Sandhill Island, and that's where she went. But that's just rumor."

Franks tried not to flinch. He had her. She lived on Sandhill Island just across the water by ferry. He could talk to her. He'd go now, but he knew the ferry didn't run at night. He'd wait until his next day off, and then he'd make a trip. "Thanks for the tip, man." He took a long and satisfying draw on the beer in celebration, then sat it down on the bar along with a five-dollar bill, tipped his hat, and left the bar.

Chapter 9

The key turned with a squeak as Neil opened his mail box. He'd walked to the community mail box center where neighbors often met and chatted on the benches set under the awning. There were public bathrooms and trashcans in the new little oasis and the island kept it clean and tidy. He pulled his mail from the box and found the packet from the attorney. The divorce was final, evidenced by the file-stamp on the top of the document they both signed, and about time. It took a year out of his life. Without thinking, he scratched his neck where the barely visible scar rubbed his collar. He seldom wore collars these days. T-shirts were just fine for his lifestyle.

The tall, thin, dark-haired woman walked his way, hips swaying the long flowing skirt that blew lightly in the breeze. He thought at first she walked barefoot, and then caught sight of the flip flops—something he still had not mastered except on the beach. Tennis shoes adapted to his style. Then he realized he'd seen her before—the jazz singer from the club. And he also remembered the warning from the shrimper that she was delicate. He understood that more than he ever thought he would. Life could reach up and smack you in the face when you weren't ready.

"Good morning." Neil nodded to the woman who approached the mail boxes lined up under the awning.

"Morning." She spoke quietly and ducked her head shyly opening her box, pulling a few items out. She then relocked it and pocketed the key.

He needed to meet the people he lived with daily on the island. He wasn't a hermit, and he still had a long life to live—he thought.

"Neil Towers," he said holding out his hand to the shy woman. She looked up at him through dark, thick eyelashes and smiled slightly.

"Billie Stone." She barely touched his hand and then withdrew.

"You're the jazz singer at Le Chez? I caught your act the other night. You have a wonderful voice." The paperwork in his hand seemed to burn next to his skin. He wasn't hitting on her, just being friendly, he reminded himself. But he found it hard to ignore her fragile kind of beauty.

"Thank you. I saw you in the restaurant. I know most of the people around here, and you were new." She thumbed through her mail.

"Snow bird—I guess. Or maybe permanent tourist. I don't know yet." True statement, since he had no idea where he might go next.

"Must be nice to be so free." She flipped open the magazine.

"Well, I guess. Like I said, I don't know yet. I have a boat down in the marina, and I live on it at the moment. Thinking about touring the gulf and maybe the Caribbean." He knew he talked too much. Maybe he needed work on his social skills.

She smiled again glancing up from her mail. "Well, it was nice to meet you, Neil." And she walked away.

"And you, Billie." He tried not to stare at the way

the skirt swayed in the breeze. Flip flops, he needed to try to master them. Islanders wore them, and he needed to fit in around here. He took the packet from the attorney and resisted the urge to toss it in the trash. He might need it later.

He dialed the office to check in on his way back to the marina. They got a little excited if he didn't talk to them now and then. But he knew his best friend, Mike, would just show up on the dock where he moored his boat if he didn't call now and then.

Mike and Neil worked together for a long time. Neil had the ideas and Mike the business sense that made the money. Neil owned an off-site IT business for offices that didn't have their own in-house staff. The bigger corporations had information technology at their fingertips. The smaller guys didn't, and they needed computer help too sometimes. Then Neil was needed. He started the business on a shoe string, getting contracts all over town, and when it became impossible to handle all the contracts alone, he hired help. Soon he needed a business manager before the monster got so big it took over everything—including his home life. Maybe he made that decision too late—at least for Allison, his ex—but Mike took on the business end and whipped it into shape.

"Hey, Mike, what's the weather like up there?" He smiled knowing how cold it could get in Billings, Montana this time of year. "That cold, huh? Here? Around 70 with a light breeze. I could fix you up with a beer and some fishing if you come down. Oh, you have to work? Would the boss know if you played hooky?" He laughed out loud. He had to say it felt good to have a good belly laugh even at his friend's expense.

Mike would come down in a heartbeat though if he thought Neil was in trouble. Mike found him that night. Saved his life actually. Not long after Allison dumped him Neil started drinking to excess—and then the suicide attempt. Dumb now that he thought about it, but at the time it seemed like a good idea. Just end it all and never have to worry or be hurt again. All those months of therapy made him realize that everyone hits bottom sometimes, and everyone has a chance to come back to the surface if they want to. He wanted to.

Yeah, he owed Mike everything. Maybe he should make sure he got a good vacation.

"I think you should seriously come down here. Leave Leanne in charge for a week and come visit. You could stay on the boat with me and get a little tan. I'm starting to look like a local—except for the flip flops." He looked at his feet.

He laughed again. "Well, think about it, bud. After tax season, put a plane ticket on your expense account. I'll approve it. You can live the life of a pirate for a week, and I'll show you around."

May seemed a long time off, and despite the beautiful scenery, Neil found he was getting lonely.

****

The trash can smelled rancid—even to a dog—at least at the bottom where she stood—but she knew there were better scraps on the top. Her long brown-colored brindle nose lifted and sniffed the air around the can when the door opened. The man in the white jacket brought her scraps and treated her kindly. She felt hungry all the time these days, and the restaurant had food. The man stepped out. He placed the pan on the ground and talked softly to her as she ate ravenously. Then he dumped the water bowl with dead insects floating in it and took it inside only to return with it holding clean, fresh, cool water.

Not all people were as kind as the man in the white jacket. She remembered being shoved roughly out of the car before it sped away leaving her behind. She chased the car to the water, but could not catch up for the traffic. Then she watched as it floated away on the ferry with the other cars. She roamed the streets at night looking for food and sleeping in alleyways, hiding from the lights. Her stomach often rumbled, and then she met the man who fed her.

She lapped the water like she licked the pan clean of scraps and raised her head, water dripping from her long snout. She was skinny. Her ribs showed that she had been a stray for a while, but the kind man fed her now. She licked his hand as he squatted down to pat her head. Just recently she allowed him to get this close. She trusted him and his scraps to be there every day and had become dependent upon them both.

"We need to find you a good home, pretty lady." The man spoke as she lapped the water again. "I don't know how you ended up on this island. But you're here now, and you need a place to live."

****

Old Poppy stepped out of the shadows with a plate in his hand. Poppy had lived on Sandhill Island longer than anyone could remember. He was a fixture. Not homeless, he had an apartment on the other side of the island that had been fixed up after the last hurricane by the trust that kept the harbor repaired. He'd helped Jon and Meg Stanford solve the murder of Jon's father and for that they were eternally grateful. And they helped him as much as he would allow. But Poppy was proud. Jon would have hired him full time, but he refused. He kept to himself. A minimalist, he needed little, but he wasn't afraid of hard work. If he needed something he would work for it, and everyone on the island kept an eye on him. He also kept an eye on his neighbors and would be there in a flash if he could help.

"That's some good fish there, Sam." He wiped his mouth with his sleeve and held out the empty plate to Sam. The dog tried to nose it. The old man leaned down and patted her head. "Can I help with those dishes tonight?"

"No, Poppy, not tonight. You go on home. I saw your limp starting up again when you came in the door. How's that hip?"

"Oh, okay. It hurts more when I've been sittin', and you know I have to sit to fish."

"Well, you come by anytime. And when that hip is better, I'll find some dirty dishes for you. Right now, the Smith kid needs a weekend job and is washing the dishes most of the time. Got to make some money for college you know."

"Well, that's right friendly of you, Sam. And you let me know when you have something for me to do." Poppy limped off down the street into the night waving goodbye over his shoulder.

"Anytime, Poppy. I always have more than enough food for everyone and could stand to take off a few pounds myself."

Chapter 10

The loud crash woke Billie from a deep sleep. Her foggy brain again thought of the car crash that trapped her inside it. Her moist skin stuck to the sheets that enveloped her, but she quickly realized she had been dreaming. She was not inside the death trap with her family. Her therapist's words came back to her to breathe and realize it was a dream, not reality. She need not be afraid of a dream. She breathed deeply.

The sky began to pink-up in the east and it would be awhile before actual sunlight overtook the island. She loved this time of day.

Then she heard it again. The wind must have picked up during the night knocking over the trash can behind the house. She unwound herself from the sheets and sat on the edge of the bed with her feet on the floor. Flip flops were left by the bed from the night before, and she slid into them. Pulling the afghan off the end of the bed, she wrapped it around her shoulders, then tip-toed to the back door careful not to wake her mother.

The trash can lay on its side moving in the wind. She opened the back door slowly, so the squeak did not wake the household, and stepped out onto the steps when she realized the air around her stood deathly still—but the can moved. She froze instantly and then saw a long slender brown tail sticking out of the can that lay on its side. She knew a stray dog had been on the island lately and Sam, the chef at Le Chez, fed it.

The tail grew larger as the dog backed out of the can toward the door—a pork chop bone in its mouth. Then it noticed her and ran for the front of the house on long thin legs. The island seldom had stray dogs because of its size, and most people with pets kept them in their yards. How this one ended up here was anyone's guess. But they would have to do a better job of securing trash or it would be all over the place. The dog needed food, even though Sam fed it all the time. And pork chop bones were irresistible. If you were a dog.

She placed the trash can back in its spot, walked back into the house and turned on the coffee pot that Raven prepared after dinner each night. With the flip of a button, a stream of aromatic brown liquid poured into the carafe. Billie inhaled deeply the aroma of morning coffee in her kitchen and salt air flowing in through open windows.

****

The brown brindle dog didn't run far with the bone. She had made a new home under the porch in the front of the house. So far, no one had spotted her. Lying on her ever-increasing belly, she crawled under the porch and lay happily chewing the bone. A great find.

Soon she would have to dig the sand out a little more as her belly lay on the ground wiggling under her. No matter how much she ate, she felt hungry. The sun came up, and the warmth shown through the boards where she lay. She dozed in the slatted rays, the bone between her feet, and dreamed doggie dreams of running through sun drenched fields chasing rabbits as the house stirred above her.

Flies buzzed around the bone and lit on her nose, waking her from a sound slumber. She rolled to her side to allow room for her girth and looked out into the distance at the shore and birds running to and fro. She was hungry once more.

Chapter 11

Sandy would be back next week—she'd promised. The kids went to see their dad for a few weeks when school let out and Sandy would come to Sandhill Island without them for a while. Billie loved to see Sandy's kids but still looked forward to some girl-time. She allowed these thoughts to interrupt her meditation.

She breathed deeply and stacked the stones one on top of the other slowly exhaling as she released each one. At the same time, she released the pain in her heart. Each stone she stacked lightened the burden within. Sometimes it worked better than others.

Today she was easily distracted. A crab walked toward her on the sand—or away from her—hard to tell with crabs who always walked sideways, but she watched its movements to and away from the water, afraid to get its feet wet. Funny little creatures who lived on the beach but were afraid of water.

And then she saw him. The man she met at the post office boxes the other day walked her way. He had a fishing pole and bagged chair over one shoulder, a tackle box in his other hand. He waved one handed with difficulty as he set up the folding chair then tripped setting down his precious cargo. With difficulty, he kept from falling. He looked up red-faced and Billie tried not to giggle.

"Flip flops!" He pointed to his feet.

She wasn't going to get anywhere with her meditation today anyway. She stood, rolling up her mat and placing it back in the bag. She walked his way smiling. "What about flip flops?"

"I don't know how you people live in them." He picked one up off the ground, brushing the sand from it and placing it back on his foot.

"I think it is a learned behavior. Actually, we put them on our babies at birth." Billie giggled again and covered her mouth with her hand.

"You have a nice laugh. You can tell a lot about a person's laugh." He took off his sunglasses and put them on top of the hat on his head. "And about their voice. Where did you learn to sing like that?"

Billie could feel her face warm with embarrassment. People often asked that question, so why did she blush when he asked? "I started singing as a kid in church, and it just progressed from there."

"A natural, huh?"

"Well, I had some instruction. My mother loved the arts and wanted me to succeed so she scraped together the money for lessons.

"Your mother is a singer too?"

"Dancer. She danced as the principal ballerina in the Corpus Christi ballet, a long time ago. Now she has Parkinson's and has lost the use of her legs." Billie brushed the hair from her face.

"That's really sad. Someone like that without her legs."

"She has a good attitude. She says she's lucky. Most people never danced on a stage, and she has her memories to sustain her. I know it hurts her though."

"I'm sure it would." Neil stared at the woman in

front of him. "What were you doing anyway?" He nodded to the rolled-up mat in her hand.

"Yoga and meditation every morning. The sea helps me concentrate so I do it on the beach. I could do it at home, but it is not as relaxing as it is with the sound of the waves coming and going."

"Meditation, huh? Is that a Buddhist thing? I've got to admit I know nothing about it, and what do the rocks have to do with it?" He placed the tackle box in the chair.

"Meditation has been around for thousands of years in several cultures, but the rocks are more a Zen thing. You stack the stones, carefully controlling your breathing with each placement. My therapist suggested it, and to tell you the truth, I thought it silly at first, but it seems to help." Billie thought she saw him flinch at the word therapist. People didn't always know how to react to therapy.

"I am sorry to hear about your family. Paul Smith told me about the accident. I asked about you when I first heard you sing."

"Paul is a wonderful man. He is my friend's uncle." She shifted her weight to the other foot, fixing the crooked sandal. "And he never met a stranger. If you want to know what's happening on the island, he is the man to talk to." She laughed again.

"He's a talker, all right. By the way, do you fish? Do you want to? I've got more equipment on the boat and could fix you up with a line sometime."

"Maybe some other time. Thanks. I need to get back and check on Mom. She has a nurse, but the poor woman needs to go home now and then. But it was nice talking to you." She meant that. She liked talking to him. Billie shifted the bag on her shoulder and walked away.

"Don't forget your rocks," he shouted over the sound of the waves.

Billie turned back to the man with the fishing rod. "You can keep them. The ocean always has more." She waved and left.

Neil watched her hips sway as she walked away, turned back to the stones stacked on the sea shore, and reached down. He pocketed the stones she had touched, and they still felt warm from her hand.

Chapter 12

The old Chevy groaned as it maneuvered onto the ferry next to minivans full of excited kids. School out, families took vacations. Joe Franks was not a fan of kids—or families for that matter. He could not wait to leave the family he grew up in as soon as possible. Dad drove a truck, and Mom was never home, leaving him at the mercy of an older brother. Kids could look cute, but looks could be deceiving.

Franks was also not a big fan of water and the waves that rolled to and fro. He could not imagine being out on the ocean unable to see land. Man should not live without his feet on dry land. He knew it to be a fact. He could see land behind him and in front, and the land in front got closer—thank goodness.

He rolled the creaky old car, and equally bald tires, off the ferry and turned left toward what appeared to be the tiny town of Sandhill Island. The rows of beach houses were peeling and in need of paint. Some looked like a tiny gust would blow them over. He moved through town and toward the shore on the outside of the island and saw a magnificent home in the distance. It had the look of an Italian villa. He wondered who would build a house so close to the water to be battered by the sea and hit by a hurricane at any time and destroyed. They must have more money than he did. Behind it sat a lush garden lined with stones that wove intricate patterns among the plants.

Passing the villa, he took the road that led to a harbor where boat slips were lined up in a row, and yachts and smaller boats floated peacefully. The island, a long thin strip of sand once part of the mainland, could be eroded away again if they weren't careful. The road turned back right toward the ferry, and there sat the restaurant. Le Chez. The only restaurant he had seen that wasn't a burger or fish-n-chips joint. It had a deck built on one side and windows that faced the water. It looked like a place a singer would hang out, not like the places he ate back in Corpus Christi. He would be back for the evening meal and entertainment. But for now, he'd visit the downtown area. As he drove past the restaurant, he noticed a small garden outback tended by a man in an open white jacket. He stood and wiped the sweat from his brow.

When evening came, Franks pulled into the almost empty restaurant parking lot. Either everyone on the island walked to Le Chez, or it was not full tonight. It smelled fishy inside. Not that he ate out that often, but when he did, the menu didn't include garlic and herbs from a garden out back. The garlic in the pizza joint came from a package. And they could keep that fishy smell, for all he cared.

"I want to sit on the patio," he said to the maître d' when approached. The man led him out the door. Here the fish and garlic smell didn't make him want to puke, blown away by the sea breeze. He sat at a table near the back. Though it was nearly dark, Franks kept on the hat and sunglasses he wore that evening. The waiter arrived with a tray containing a basket of bread and glass of ice water with a wedge of lemon perched on top. He assumed they were free. The waiter handed him a menu. Franks grumbled under his breath. This would take everything he made in tips that evening and then some.

And then she appeared; belting out a song Franks didn't know. Her voice like thick honey oozing out of a bottle—warm and never ending. And he began to feel a little sorry for the woman with the golden voice. But he quickly squelched such feelings.

"Do you have a burger?" The waiter pointed to the menu and Franks snorted. "Highway robbery. I guess that's what I'll have." He handed back the menu.

"Would you like to substitute sweet potato fries, sir?"

"Is it extra?" The waiter nodded. "Then no, just plain." Franks had never eaten fried sweet potatoes. His grandmother made pies of them sometimes, but he wasn't paying extra for anything.

The restaurant began to clear out and the busboys cleaned up quickly, hoping to go home early. Billie finished the song she performed and then thanked everyone for coming. Franks looked around, one rowdy table up front still drinking. The waiter came by refusing another round. One man sat alone off to the side.

Franks had long since quit on the huge burger and asked for a carry out box. The food was good after all; he didn't want it to go to waste. A big change from the left-over pizza people failed to pick up that often made his evening meal.

The tall black man with the bass fiddle put up the cords and stowed the equipment as Billie put down the mic and closed the piano. They were done for the evening. She spoke quietly to the man on the stage with her, gave a small wave at the man who sat off to the side, then left the tiny stage.

Franks stood as she walked toward the door to the restaurant. He laid some bills on the table and followed her—food box in hand. She stopped at the kitchen as he left through the front door to wait for her.

Standing in the dark by his car he watched as she stepped from the restaurant, kicked off her shoes and stepped into flip flops. She pushed the hair from her face as she looked up into the night sky. She probably never thought about security on Sandhill Island. Franks doubted that the police ever came around.

He stepped out of the shadows and walked toward her. "Ms. Stone?" She turned with a jerk. "I'm sorry, I didn't mean to frighten you." He took another step toward her. "I just wanted to say how much I enjoyed the performance tonight." He smiled a greasy smile. She stepped back.

"Um, thank you." She started to turn and walk away. He stepped closer.

"I wanted to talk with you, if I may." He reached for her arm.

"Don't touch me!" She flinched and backed up. Then she stopped. "Do I know you?"

"Yes, we've met." He took off the hat and rubbed his hand through his hair. Then slid the sunglasses down his nose and looked at her over the rim. "Joe Franks."

She took another step back. "What do you want? And how did you find me?"

"It's not hard to find someone as famous as you."

She reached for the door handle. "Go away before I

call the police."

"What police? On this little dump of an island?"

"We have constables. We're not without protection." She opened the door and called, "String! Sam!"

"Now don't get excited. I only wanted to talk."

"I have nothing to say to you." Billie hugged the door facing.

"Look, I just thought, I've paid my debt to society, and maybe you could help me find a job. Besides, I'm broke because of you." Franks tried to keep the pleading out of his voice.

"String!" she shouted again, and the tall dark man stuck his head out the door, followed by the chef Franks saw earlier—and the man from the other table.

"Why would I help you? You killed my family."

"It was an accident and besides, I served my time." He took the sunglasses off, and this time he backed up as the big bass player walked out the door.

"One year! One year! Is that all that two lives are worth? One year for two lives. My baby is dead, he'll never grow up and have a life of his own. And my husband—a good family man—cut down in the prime of his life and you want my help?" Billie's voice screamed louder.

"What's going on here?" the tall man in the Hawaiian shirt stepped closer. He looked at Franks. "I don't know who you are or what you want, but you better be leaving Ms. Stone alone. We're pretty fond of her around here and don't like strangers messing with her." Then he stopped as the reality sank in. "Joe Franks? Joe Franks? What the fuck are you doing here?"

How did he know his name? "I'm talking to Billie. It's really none of your concern." Franks used his bravest voice sounding more confident than he felt. He had seen this man before. Maybe in the court room during the trial.

"Anything having to do with Ms. Stone is my concern." The tall man stepped toward Franks.

The door opened more widely, and the chef walked out along with Neil Towers.

"You're the cheapskate griping about the prices, aren't you?" The man in the white chef jacket that he had seen earlier in the day gestured to Franks. "Well go on and get out. We don't allow arguments in the parking lot of this establishment. Now you go on and get home." He nodded at Franks.

"I don't have to leave a public parking place." Franks stood his ground.

Sam punched the numbers into the cell phone. "I'm calling the police."

String rushed forward, grabbing Franks by his arm making him drop the expensive burger, and pushed him roughly toward the only car left in the parking lot. "Get out of here and don't come back. 'Cause if you do, the cops will be waiting. I'd like nothing more than to make you disappear off a pier somewhere, but I'll settle for putting you back in prison for a while. Now don't let me find you back on Sandhill Island again. Ever. Do you hear?"

The door handle of Franks' car dug into his back. He looked at Billie. "All I wanted was a letter of recommendation from you. I did my time and paid your bills. It seemed the least you could do for ruining my life. I can't find a decent job…"

"She ruined your life? What do you think you did? Now get out of here and don't come back!" String yanked opened the door, pushed him in, and slammed it shut behind him. Franks started the engine of his jalopy and gunned it once then backed out, slinging sand as he spun tires and drove away.

Billie stood sobbing, Sam patting her shoulder.

"Who was that?" Neil Towers stepped to the other side of Billie.

"Never mind." Sam and String said in unison. "I'll take her home." String put his big arm around her and they walked off together. "When the cops get here, send them to the house," he called over his shoulder

"I'm sorry, I didn't mean to intrude. I just hated seeing Billie so upset," Neil said to Sam as they walked back in the restaurant.

"It's okay." Sam sighed. "That's the guy who caused the accident that killed her family. What he is doing here and how he found her is the question."

"Well, I didn't mean to get in the way. She's a great lady, and I don't want to see her hurt. I also need to pay someone for my meal."

Sam gestured to the waiter. "Thanks for your concern, Neil. But we'll take care of Billie."

****

Outside the dog sniffed the take-out container with the burger and trotted off behind the restaurant with the foam box in her teeth.

Once home, Billie guided String to the porch swing.

"Let me get my wits about me before I go in." Billie once again wiped her eyes with her hands as the door to the house opened and Raven walked out.

72

"Is everything okay?" She walked toward Billie as the constable's car drove up.

"Joe Franks came to the restaurant tonight to talk to me."

"Oh, good Lord! Honey, are you okay? Can I get you something?" Raven patted Billie's hands as they lay in her lap. "How about some tea?"

Billie nodded.

The constable took the report and then stated he could do little, but he would look the guy up in the probation records.

"I'll check to see if there is still a restraining order. If not, you might have to have one set up again." The man in the navy-blue uniform wrote notes on the pad from his pocket.

"I think it lapsed after he went to prison," Billie lifted the tea cup to her lips with shaking hands as she sat on the swing, the constable stood by making notes. String had moved to a nearby chair, and Raven took his place.

"And I think you need to call the doctor in the morning. This was a big shock." String looked at her like a big brother. Again, Billie nodded.

After everyone left, Raven helped her to bed, and Billie lay staring out the window at the moon. Why did she keep reliving the nightmare of her family's death, she wondered as she dozed off?

The next morning Billie found a long lanky man curled up uncomfortably on her porch swing snoring. String had spent the night watching over her as usual.

Chapter 13

Barefoot, with the yoga mat and flip flops in hand, Billie eased open the screen door and slipped out quietly. She might need extra meditation this morning after a fitful and almost sleepless night.

Seagulls soared overhead, and the sea breeze blew back the hair from her face. No matter what life threw at her, Billie could count on the ocean to sooth her nerves. She walked to the rocky shore at the other end of the island without thinking—and there he sat.

Neil Towers sat on the rocks, fishing pole in hand. He looked out to sea oblivious of her arrival. She almost turned back. But this was where she practiced meditation, and he could leave. She was staying.

"Good morning," he said without turning when her shadow peeked over his shoulder. She placed the yoga mat on the ground beside the rocks. "Am I bothering you? Because if I am, I can move."

"No, of course not. Stay. It's a big ocean." Billie took the sunglasses off her face.

"I knew you would be here, and I wanted to make sure you were okay after last night." He spoke with his back to her.

"Really, I'm fine." She walked to the water's edge beside the boulders and looked for small stones to stack later.

"You have a great support group here on the island

with String and Sam. But I wanted to throw my hat in the ring too. If you need anything—ever—I wanted you to know that I'm here for you."

"That's very kind, but unnecessary." Billie walked back to the yoga mat.

"Well, I'm not going to ask any questions. Just know, if Sam or String are not around, I will be. My boat is in the harbor and going nowhere soon. I have nothing to do but fish all day and I'm around if you need me." He turned and looked into her eyes still swollen from the crying fit last night. "I brought you coffee." He handed her the Styrofoam cup that sat beside him as he drank the other. "I didn't know how you took it, so it's black."

Her hands trembled as she took the cup. "Thank you. You're very kind." She walked down the beach a few feet and spread the yoga mat, laid the stones beside it, and picked up the ear buds. "I couldn't believe he found me. And then I really couldn't believe he blamed me for his problems in life. He said he wanted me to write him a letter of recommendation! I'll recommend he get life in prison if he likes." She started to shake, took a deep breath and let it out slowly.

"He obviously has no remorse." Neil put his pole into a crack between the rocks and stood. "Paul and Sam told me a little about the accident; they also said you were fragile, and I should keep my distance from you. They thought I might make matters worse for you. But I want you to know, that's not my intention. I'm here to start a new life too. Here to heal. My wife divorced me, and I went a little crazy, hit the bottle too much, and even attempted suicide." He pulled down the neckline of his T-shirt showing her the scar that ran around his neck. "A friend found me. I know a little about therapy and coming back from the brink. Not like you do, but I wanted you to know, you are not alone. There are a lot of us out there trying to put our lives back together, and it seems to me that helping each other is why we were put on this earth. So, if you need anything, or just need to talk, or just need me to shut up and go away, say so."

Billie sniffed and wiped her eyes with the back of her hand, took a sip of the coffee, and looked out to sea. "Thank you. I had no idea. I know I'm not alone in the world. I have my mom and friends, but it has been very hard. I came home to heal, and then Mom got sick, and I got another kick in the gut. My therapist said yoga and meditation would help. And they do." She turned and looked at Neil. "I could teach you if you want." She smiled through tear-stained eyes.

"I don't know if I can twist this body into a pretzel or not." Neil looked down at the mat that lay on the sand. "I think my meditation is at the end of a fishing pole."

"Okay. Maybe later. I'm just going to plug in and practice a few poses if you don't mind—and I think there might be something nibbling on your line." Billie nodded to the pole sliding toward the water.

"Crap!" Neil lunged for the pole, grabbing it and reeling in the line which went taut—and then slack—as the fish swam away with his bait. "Well, so much for that one, but I'll get the next one."

Billie hid a smile with her hand and then sat on the mat, plugged into the soothing music and began her morning routine.

Deep into her practice she barely noticed Neil

76

slipping away.

Pulling the earbuds from her ears, she reached for the stones when a large shadow loomed over her.

"How you doing, girl?" String stood with one hand up to shade his eyes and the other on the small of his back.

"Probably better than you. Did you sleep on the swing all night?"

"Slept some, swung back and forth a lot. Did you know you have a dog under your house?"

"A dog?" Billie carefully balanced the last stone on the top.

"Yeah, I think it is the mutt that has been hanging out at the restaurant. And I think she may be pregnant. I watched her dig out a little more sand and scoot underneath. You may be having puppies one of these days."

"Well, I don't need a dog or certainly a litter of puppies. We need to find her a home." Billie stood and rolled up the yoga mat, brushing the sand from underneath.

"Thanks again for staying last night. I called my doctor and have an appointment on the mainland. I need to get a shower and get going before I'm late." She touched his arm as she walked past.

"Sure. I'm glad you're seeing the doctor today after what happened last night. Maybe she has some good advice about handling the situation. She has always been good for you. I'll see you later." He waved as he walked away toward his apartment.

Chapter 14

The office always smelled of lavender. The diffuser that sat in the corner was meant to help the client relax. Unless the client hated the smell of lavender. Which she didn't. What if somebody was allergic to lavender? She wasn't. Billie's thoughts were jumbled this morning, and she knew she needed to concentrate. Lavender wasn't the issue. She breathed deeply and instinctively crossed her legs into a lotus pose on the couch. Two years ago, that would never have occurred to her.

Dr. Nicole Flint took the seat opposite her with notebook in hand. Imagine what all that notebook had heard! Literally pages and pages of lives and their secrets went into a notebook transcribed into files for each client.

The doctor, in black palazzo pants and white knit top, sat with legs crossed at the knees and swept her short dark hair behind one ear. "So, tell me what's been going on."

Instinctively Billie began to tear up. How many times had she cried on this woman's shoulder? She must be sick of her constant whining by now. But the doctor never acted that way. She found her always soothing and comforting—until she held a mirror up for Billie to see herself and then things could get ugly.

"Well, Joe Franks is out of prison." Billie brushed

a piece of lint from her pants.

"Yes, we knew that." The doctor raised one eyebrow in question.

"And he came to see me at the restaurant."

"Is the protective order still in place?" The doctor looked up from her notebook.

"I don't know. I don't think so. He went to prison, so it wasn't needed anymore, and who knew he'd ever want to see me again? I mean the courts initially set it up because he started calling me when he made bail. But after he went to prison, I thought that would be the end of him. He only spent a year in jail, and now he's out. He said he wanted me to help him get a job. He said the restitution program broke him because of me. Well, I'm broke too, especially emotionally. I mean where does he get off?" The words rolled from her mouth like the flood gates had been opened. Once she started, she could hardly stop.

"Well, it needs to be reinstated. You can get your lawyer to do that for you or you can do it yourself." The doctor eyed her closely. "Would that help to make you feel safe?"

"I suppose it would. But what good is a piece of paper if he really has something in mind? I mean he said he wanted me to write him a letter of recommendation, that he had paid his debt to society. He will never repay the debt of my family being gone. That is not possible. He was sentenced to one year for involuntary manslaughter. One year! My family is dead, and he got one year." Billie grabbed a tissue from the box on the table next to the couch and blew her nose loudly. "He's the reason I'm here. He's the reason I have nightmares."

"How are the nightmares?" Dr. Flint took off her glasses and looked at Billie with clear blue eyes.

"Actually, they're better. I seldom have them. I did have one last night, but I slept so little it hardly mattered."

"So, you think the medication and yoga are helping?"

"Yes, normally they do. Last night I felt different. It was such a shock, and just the idea that he thought I should help him took me by surprise. I wasn't scared so much as angry."

"I think anger is a step forward. It could be healing. Anger is a very real emotion, and if channeled correctly, could help you deal with all you have going on. It is a natural adaptive response; when you feel threatened, anger helps you to feel empowered. You need to feel empowered, Billie. You have suffered a great loss, and like we talked about, you will always feel that loss. But you can also feel that you are in charge of your life. Anger can give you the courage to defend yourself. You need to be able to feel you can defend yourself and feel like less of a victim. You need to ask yourself what is within your control. And then you need to act on it." The doctor continued to look at Billie. The room deathly still, except for the soft hiss of the diffuser.

Billie nodded and cleared her throat. "I wanted to tell you I met a new friend on the island. Neil Towers is a snow bird from Montana, and he lives on his boat. He seems a little smitten with me. He's a nice man even though I'm not looking for one. Anyway, he told me his wife divorced him, and he attempted suicide. He wanted me to know I wasn't alone, I think. He has had a lot of counseling, and now he lives here. I don't think he wants to go home." Billie shifted in her seat.

"How do you feel about his attention toward you?" Dr. Flint looked up from her writing.

"Well, like I said, I'm not looking for a boyfriend. I'll just keep it friendly. I'm not sure I'm a good match for anyone right now, maybe never."

"And what do we say to accept?" The doctor looked at her closely.

"I need to accept my imperfections." Billie repeated the mantra as if she were a child in the classroom. They always said that at the end of a session. A good thing to remember, if she could actually do it.

"Good. A new friend is a good thing. A romantic entanglement might prove challenging, but you never know. You need to lean on yourself, Billie, not someone else. Just remember you are strong on your own—strong enough to support yourself. And if you want a relationship, you are strong enough for that too. As long as he is not dependent. Get the protective order against Joe Franks reinstated. It is a shield, especially if the police get involved. After all, he's still on probation. He's barely out of jail, and he still needs to feel like a prisoner for a while. He wants to blame his problems on someone, and you are his target. Don't let him make you a victim.

"What do you think is driving the anger you feel against Joe Franks? What is underneath it?" The therapist pointed to Billie with her glasses.

"I don't know. I think I believed him to be sorry for what he did. He admitted remorse in open court. But now, I feel betrayed. I know he can't bring them back, but he could at least feel badly about taking lives." Billie sobbed again.

"Okay, good. You know where the anger is coming from. Now I want you to write down what you feel and bring it with you next time. I want to see you again next week. Let's discuss this anger issue then and see if we can help you feel less victimized. Don't forget to take care of the protective order."

"No, I won't forget. I'll get on it in the morning. Thank you."

Billie made the appointment with the receptionist and dropped the card in her purse on the way out the door. She really did feel better.

Chapter 15

At the turnstile, the bags flowed in and then back out—all the same—all black. The only thing different were the name tags attached. Neil and Mike stood mesmerized watching for just the right bag at Corpus Christi International.

"How about some dinner before we go to the boat?" Neil turned to his friend in the passenger seat of the convertible. The bag in the trunk, they pulled out of the parking space at the airport.

"I thought you were feeding me fish at your place."

"Only if you catch it." Neil smiled at his friend.

"Well, if that's the case, I might lose some weight while I'm here. Maybe we should check out the local restaurants."

Pulling the sports car into a parking lot of a local chain, Neil stepped out of the Mercedes. "Well, there aren't a lot of places to eat on the island, but there is one nice restaurant I want to take you to. There is a woman who sings the blues there, and you have to hear her."

"A woman, huh?" Mike eyed his friend.

"Not like that. She is a fantastic singer and has a story. I'll tell you all about her over a burger, okay?"

Stuffed after the burger, they drove toward the island barely making the last call at the ferry.

"Really, you get there by ferry? I mean, were you

trying to get away from the world?" Mike stood at the railing looking out at the strand of water that ran between the mainland and Sandhill Island.

"Yeah, I think so. But this place…" Neil looked across the water. "There is something soothing about this place. I can't put my finger on it, but I love it here."

"Well, you're not going into the office every day, so that may be what you love."

"I was never afraid of hard work. I just went over the edge after the divorce and took a little detour on the way back home." Neil laughed at his own joke. He knew it to be true. "The island closes down at night since the ferry quits running, and things really grind to a halt. And that's all right with me."

They drove off the ferry and turned right toward the harbor. "I'll give you the grand tour in the morning when you can see better. But here is my little home-away-from-home." He pointed to the slip with the boat gently swaying in the lapping water. It read *Overboard* on the stern in script.

"*Overboard*. I like it." Mike climbed out of the car and walked to the trunk for his bag.

"Told you she was a beauty." Neil put the top up on the car and locked it then walked down the gangplank to the slip he rented. Climbing in, he turned and took the bag from his friend. "Welcome aboard." He smiled and tossed the bag to a seat.

"How about a cold one? There are twin beds in the hull, little close quarters, but it works."

Grabbing the bag, Mike followed Neil inside.

"You can have that one," he said gesturing to the bed on the right. "It has clean sheets and everything." Then walked to the kitchen and took two beers from the refrigerator. "Let's go up top with these."

****

"Sandy's coming tomorrow. The kids went to Dad's for a few weeks after school let out, and she's coming to spend the week with her mom." Billie pocketed the cell phone and turned to her mother sitting in the wheel chair.

"Again? That's great. She must be homesick."

"I think she is getting tired of the job—being away from home all the time and such. I think the excitement is growing thin with her. She said she had something else in mind." Billie walked toward the chair that her mother lived in these days. She wondered if her attitude would be as good if she had a similar fate.

"Well, you should not be held down by your job. I assume she has to keep the kids in Mississippi though, since their dad is there." Giselle sat up straight in her chair looking out the window.

"Probably. She mentioned something about teaching. There are colleges there, and she might be able to do something else. She's earned it."

"I'm sure she has." Giselle looked out to sea through the window that had just been cleaned. "How about some tea?" She turned and looked at her daughter.

"Of course, hot or iced?" Billie put her hands on the handle of the chair and pushed her mother toward the door.

"Hot, I think. I'm a little chilly this morning." The older woman reached her gnarled hand up and buttoned the top button on her robe.

Chapter 16

She woke with a start when the ladder hit the side of the house. Martha Smith, Sandy's mother, threw open the bedroom door pulling on a cotton bathrobe.

"Morning Mom!" Sandy stood drinking her second cup of coffee.

"Sandy? What is that noise?" Martha ran for the front door.

"It's okay, Mom, it's just the painters." Sandy walked from the kitchen barefoot with a coffee cup in her hand.

"The what? I don't have painters coming. I wish I did, but I can't afford to pay someone to paint this house." She looked at her daughter who stood leaning on the door facing with a knowing smile on her face.

"Sandra Louise, what have you done?" She eyed her daughter who stared back with a smug look on her face.

"Just what needed to be done that I didn't have time to do myself. I hired a painter. They are going to scrape today. And I hope you liked the color, I ordered yellow with white trim—just like it used to be."

"Well, it's not okay. I can't afford this, and you should not be paying for my house painting."

"You said the house would be mine someday, I'm just protecting it from the elements. Anyway, it needed to be done, and I wanted to do it for you. He will scrape, prime, and paint. I hope this paint job lasts longer than the last one. We'll see."

A pause hung in the air and both women stared at each other. "Sandy, Sandy, Sandy, I don't know what to say." She walked toward her daughter holding her arms out and then enfolding her in an embrace.

"Well, I didn't know they were going to wake you, sorry, but happy birthday."

"It isn't my birthday." Martha looked out the window again.

"Well, Merry Christmas?" Sandy took a sip of coffee.

"Whatever. You're a good daughter." Martha patted her shoulder. "What do you want for breakfast?" Martha walked toward the kitchen.

"I don't know, what do you have?" Sandy opened the refrigerator and took out the orange juice, pouring two glasses. She knew her mother loved orange juice in the morning.

"Omelet?" Martha pulled the eggs out and carried them to the stove.

"I love your omelets." Sandy reached back for cheese and onion and began to help her mother cook.

"Are you going to see Billie today? You know there are some new places here on the island since the tourism has increased. They put in an ice cream shop, and then there is a burger and a fish place. Just little fast food joints, but you should take her. I doubt that she gets out much except to Le Chez and home." Martha beat the eggs in a bowl.

"I hope the tourism doesn't increase too much. I would hate for this to become a spring break haven for the college kids."

"I doubt there is that much for them to do here." She poured the egg mixture into the pan.

"Well, I might just see if she wants to show me around. You want to come?" Sandy pulled two plates from the cabinet and put bread in the toaster.

"Oh, I don't know. I don't walk as well as you girls—my arthritis, you know." Martha pushed a strand of hair behind one ear.

"Well, we'll walk slow. You're welcome to come. I'm here to see my mom and Billie. And the ladders may get noisy."

Martha took the plates to the table and pulled out a chair "You know, I'm not a very good neighbor. Maybe I should visit Giselle while you girls are out. I only live a few blocks away, and it's not like I do that much. Maybe I'll bake some cookies and take them over. I have some dough in the refrigerator.". She bit into the toast with a bite of egg then stood and turned on the oven.

"I think that's a great idea, Mom." Apricot jam slid off the toast and dripped onto Sandy's plate. She scooped it up with a finger and licked it off, then took her plate to the sink. "I'm going to get a shower and then I'll do these dishes."

****

The ocean breeze blew Sandy's long blonde hair from her face as she walked in shorts and flip flops. Though the asphalt road was often invisible because of the blowing sand, the women knew the way into town. It was hard to get lost on such a small island.

"I see Sanders' Hardware is still open." Sandy pushed the sunglasses up on her head in the shade of the awning.

"I think he does well. Everyone needs hardware now and then." Billie continued to walk down the street.

The main street of the island looked like many small towns, with shops and awnings. There were T-shirt shops for the tourists and places to get in out of the sun for a cold drink. Many of the shops were damaged in the last hurricane but had been repaired. The one shop that didn't fare well was an artist's studio, now a blank spot in the road, a piece of real estate ripe for building a new place, but it sat empty with an occasional sprig of sea grass poking up out of the sand.

"The ice cream parlor went into that empty building at the end of the block. Is it too early for ice cream?" Billie pointed to the small building with lemon-yellow bistro tables sitting beside turquoise pots of blooming petunias out front, then looked at her friend.

"I'm on vacation. No work, no kids, just my best friend in the world. It's never too early for ice cream." Crossing the street, they were met by the occasional tourist with red noses and white legs. They left their desk jobs once a year for a little rest and relaxation, brought the kids and played like beach bums for a week. They were intent on having a good time—too much to eat, and too much to drink—before returning to the grind.

Inside the artificially cool shop they ordered ice cream cones, and then stepped back outside to the tables in the front. Like most mothers, Sandy instinctively picked up extra napkins and laid them on the table between them.

"I love this little town," Sandy licked the Rocky

Road, sucking out a marshmallow, and then chewing it. Rocky Road had been her favorite even as a kid. She said the marshmallows reminded her of clouds.

Billie used a spoon to pick the peach pieces from her frozen concoction, spooning them into her mouth, and then licked the cream itself. There hadn't always been an ice cream shop on the island, but they spent many summers in each other's yard licking the sticky sweetness from their fingers.

"It's funny the things that come back to you. Do you remember the block parties we used to have, and the old man who made his own ice cream? I can't remember his name." Billie licked the bottom of the waffle cone that started to drip.

"I don't remember either. But I do know where he lived. He always had the best ice cream, and Mom would bring her award-winning cookies. The same ones she took to your mom this morning." Sandy searched for the nuts frozen in the ice cream.

"They are award winning. At least in my mind. How does she get them so light and crisp? Do you think she would teach me?" Billie now sucked the melted cream from the bottom of the cone, as it dripped in earnest, then wrapped it in several layers of napkin.

"She'd love to. It would give her something to do and pass down a skill. You know she won't be around forever. Neither of them will." Sandy looked up as the Mercedes convertible pulled into the parking space in front of the ice cream shop. There were two young men in the car—snow birds. Probably here for the warmer weather and to get out of the office for a week.

"Hi, ladies, good to see you out and about." The dark-haired man behind the wheel nodded at Billie as he got out of the car.

"Hi, Neil. I see you have company." Billie smiled at the man and his guest.

"Yes, this is Mike Anderson. He's my buddy from Montana, here for the week."

"Sandy, this is Neil Towers. He owns a boat in the marina and has been coming to hear me sing. He is a fisherman who MAY learn yoga someday. And this is my friend Sandy Miller. She grew up on the island and now lives in Biloxi." Billie gestured to Sandy as she wiped the ice cream from her chin.

"Nice to meet you both." Sandy smiled around the ice cream. "I'd shake your hand, but mine is a bit sticky at the moment." Sandy noticed Billie's ease with the stranger. That had to be a move in the right direction.

"Do they have good ice cream?" Neil looked at Billie over the top of his sunglasses.

"Mine's good. They've only been opened a short time. This place needed an ice cream parlor."

"What do you say, man? Ice cream?" Neil nodded to Mike then the door of the shop. The men walked in the door.

"He seems nice." Sandy looked at Billie knowingly. "Do you think they really want ice cream or is it just an opportunity to talk to a couple of really hot girls?"

"Girls?" Billie smiled. "I think I quit being a girl a long time ago. But yes, you might be right. Neil has been very attentive lately. He brought me coffee the other day as I practiced yoga."

"I thought you didn't allow any interruptions when you practice yoga and meditation." Sandy bit the cone which collapsed into her hand. She shoved the entire thing into her mouth, barely able to close it.

"Well, there had been an incident at the restaurant the night before and he checked up on me." Billie bit into the waffle cone.

"What kind of incident?" Sandy wiped her mouth.

"The Joe Franks kind of incident."

Sandy raised her eyebrows.

"I haven't had time to tell you. He showed up at the restaurant and wanted me to write him a letter of recommendation, so he could get a better job. Now that he's served his time and all." Billie wiped the melted ice cream from the table.

"What? That worm! I didn't even realize he got out of jail. And the bigger question is, why is he out of jail? He should never get out as far as I'm concerned, but the courts felt differently."

"Well, Sam and String were there, and Neil. He wanted to help. The next morning, he sat fishing on the beach when I got there and told me his life story. Divorced, drinking and a suicide attempt. He has had a lot of therapy and he just wanted me to know I wasn't alone." Billie licked the sticky cream off her fingers and then sucked them clean.

"Well, he's right, you're not alone. But I wonder how your therapist would feel about you getting involved with someone who has had emotional problems? I mean, would it be like a crutch?" Sandy wiped her mouth again, thankful for the extra napkins.

"I don't plan to get involved with him, but he is nice, and I enjoy talking to him. I also saw my therapist that day and told her about him."

Sandy looked at her friend across the table. "I think that might be a good thing for you to come out of your shell a little and enjoy people again. Just be careful. And, don't look now, but they are coming back." She nodded slightly at the men as they walked out the door of the shop.

"Can we sit with you?" Neil asked walking up to the table.

"Of course. We're finished and about to leave anyway." Billie nodded to the empty chairs.

"Well, don't leave. We just got here." Neil looked genuinely upset that the women would not stay.

"Well, we can stay for just a minute. I'm showing Sandy around her old hometown."

"Mike and I are seeing the sites too. Do you ladies have plans for later? Could we buy you dinner or maybe just some coffee?"

Sandy could see Billie put on the brakes. "No thanks, we're just enjoying a girl's day out. But it was nice to see you." Billie rose from the table and Sandy followed. Obviously, Billie could still be scared off easily.

"Well, come down to the boat later and we'll take you for a ride." Neil looked hopeful.

"Maybe," Billie said and walked away with Sandy in tow.

"You're pushin' man." Mike said looking down at the cup of ice cream after the women left.

"I think I'm out of practice." Neil laughed and shoved the ice cream away.

Chapter 17

The dog, heavy with puppies, slid under the porch grunting as she went. The shade felt cooler there and the sea breeze blew across her nose. It told her of fish and water and kids—and also danger. Splashing through the cool water was fun chasing crabs, but these days, with her body heavy and cumbersome, play was more trouble. The waves would surely knock her down, and she might not get back up.

The puppies were her first litter. She was a nurturer by nature, even if she didn't understand the changes in her body. She felt protective of what grew inside her and consequently made her hungry all the time. The man at the restaurant fed her daily if she met him out back. He also had cool water for her to drink. But she had come to think of the porch at the little house as home. She heard the comings and goings of the people who lived in the house and knew instinctively that they were good, like the man at the restaurant, and would let her stay. And she dozed with the cool sea breeze blowing up her nose.

****

"You know that dog is back, and I think she plans to stay." Raven wiped her hands on the apron that covered her scrubs. It told of the double duty she pulled daily—that of nurse and often cook. The kitchen smelled of grilled cheese sandwiches and tomato basil soup. The soup, one of Sam's specialties, Billie brought home with her every time he made it.

"I can't stand to see her without a home. Do you know someone who would take her in?" Billie stood at the sink as the warm soapy water covered the dishes and her hands.

"Well, I can think of one person who might need her." Raven eyed Billie up and down. "You know, one of these days you'll be alone, and that dog might just be the ticket."

"Oh, I don't need a dog." Billie wiped the soap from the plate and then dunked it in the rinse water placing it in the rack to drain.

"Maybe you don't and maybe you do. I love you honey, but you know when your mother goes, I must go too. I can come back and visit, and we'll always be friends, but I'll have to move on to another job. You don't need me like your mother does." Raven picked up the dishtowel and dried the plate. "I'm just saying a companion—even the furry kind—is what you need."

"Oh, you're a psychiatrist now." Billie smiled at the nurse who often had two patients for the price of one.

"Just sayin'." Raven dried the last dish and put it in the cabinet.

The soapy water drained down the sink, and Billie wiped the cabinet top. Her mother was taking her afternoon nap, and Billie had time to herself. She walked to the bedroom and picked up the novel beside the bed, taking it to the front porch swing. Maybe a nap, or a little reading, whichever came first.

She leaned back on the pillow that cushioned the arm and drew her legs up on the other end, sliding her toes under the afghan that lay on the swing. The gentle breeze blew through the screens and gently rocked her, reminding her of why she lived here. She felt the seashore in her soul and breathed deeply, then she heard the rumblings beneath her.

The dog was back.

Billie sat up as the brown nose poked out from under the porch. The dog obviously struggled to free itself from the encumbrance. She wiggled loose and stood stretching in the sun, her soft brindle coat shining. Her girth had increased since the last time Billie had seen her. Puppies grew much faster than human babies. She took a step and sniffed the salty air, turned and looked back over her shoulder at Billie.

"Good afternoon." Billie nodded at the pregnant hound. She knew the dog had nowhere to go and would give birth to the babies where she felt safe. And she felt safe under Billie's porch.

The dog nodded back with her doggie smile and then looked out to sea. She trotted off in the direction of Le Chez for her afternoon snack. The lunch rush would be over, and Sam would take out the trash. Like it or not, Billie and Sam had a dog. They probably couldn't run her off, and Billie found she didn't want to.

Opening the screen door to the porch, Billie stepped out onto the warm sand barefoot and looked at the tiny place the dog had burrowed under. She walked to the back porch knowing she had a garden trowel there. Billie got down on her knees and began to dig out the sand where the dog made a temporary home. She would make her a bed on the porch if she liked. Maybe later she could graduate to the house. She wondered what kind of dog food a pregnant mother needed. The dog reminded Billie of herself. Raven was right, the dog needed someone, and Billie might need someone too.

It had been a long time since she had a dog in her life. She'd call her Lillie after the grandmother she never knew but her mother spoke of fondly. And she would begin to look for someone to take puppies when they were born. Of course, that would be a while. At least she thought so.

She had a dog—assuming it wanted to stay. The chances were good it wouldn't leave.

Chapter 18

Tying the apron around her, Billie gazed at Martha's spotless kitchen. Everything in place, unlike Billie's homey and warm kitchen that often looked like a tornado hit it. Clean, but cluttered.

"So, I hear you have a new pet." Martha pulled out the flour tin and blue glass mixing bowl. The shortening and sugar were within arms-length.

"Lillie. She is so sweet. Do you want a puppy? We're going to be having some soon." Billie reached for a wooden spoon in the crock nestled in the corner.

"Oh, I think I'm too old to start over with a puppy." Martha laid the recipe next to the bowl.

"Well, I felt so sorry for her when I realized she slept under the porch. I tried to make a bed for her inside, but she was having none of that. She likes being under the porch. She has dug out the sand, and I keep thinking she is going to get stuck. Her belly keeps getting bigger."

"Well, she's yours now. You feed her and give her a home, and she'll never leave." Martha handed the measuring cups to Billie.

"I'm not sure I want her to, actually. I haven't had a dog in a long time, and she's a comfort to me. Besides, she needs help—and I understand that." Billie picked up the recipe and looked at the ingredients. "We had a discussion the other night, and I told her the rules.

She doesn't eat off my plate, she has a bowl, and she is not to get run over by a car, because that would make me cry, and Lord knows I've done enough of that for a lifetime. Anyway, she promised, and we formed a human-doggie bond. I know Mom won't be around forever and when Mom goes, so does Raven, then I'm alone again." Billie measured the flour according to the recipe.

"Well, I live close. I know that Sandy won't be here all the time, but I will, and you and I can do things together, like make cookies. I can be a second mother, probably not as good as the first, but I'll be around." Martha smiled at the woman she'd known since a child.

"Martha, you're so sweet. I remember you taught me to swim. Sandy and I were playing in the water, and you came out to play with us. Mom didn't swim much, mostly just sun bathed."

"Well, you were floundering out there, and I didn't want you to step in a hole and drown three feet from shore. Now, the secret to this dough is to refrigerate it for two hours or even overnight. Then you form the dough into balls about the size of a walnut, and we'll roll them in the sugar-cinnamon mixture." She took the bowl and placed it in the refrigerator as Sandy came in the door carrying sacks.

"Hey girlfriend." She nodded at Billie and then kissed her mom on the cheek. "Okay, I hope I got everything on the list." She placed the groceries on the cabinet top and began to put away the salad greens. "I also stopped and got the things we need for a pedicure. I know there is no place around here for that, so I guess we can do it on the front porch." She reached into the bag and pulled out a bottle of nail polish and handed it to Billie.

"Lime Sherbet? We're going to have green toenails?"

"Why not. It's a beach. By the way, I ran into your boyfriend again, and he wants us to go out on his boat."

"I don't have a boyfriend." Billie eyed her friend over the nail polish bottle.

"Well, then that cute guy who keeps chasing you. Neil, I think you called him. Anyway, as I recall, we have at least two hours before we can bake cookies, so what do you say ladies—pedicure?"

"I don't know if I want green toenails, Sandy." Martha looked at her daughter. "But I think I have a pale pink in the bathroom. I'll join you out front."

Martha sat with her feet in the dishpan of warm soapy water, last in line as the women clipped, cleaned, filed and prepared their toenails for the crowning glory of color. Sandy put the final coat of Lime Sherbet on her toes and reached for the top coat to protect her art work. Billie swung in the swing with foam wedges between her toes as the color dried.

"I don't know if the Air Force would approve of this color, but they'll never see it through my flight boots." Sandy picked up her mother's foot and dried it placing it on her knee and began the process all over again. The older woman sat with her arms folded in her lap and smiled.

"So, you really think you've had enough of storm chasing?" Martha watched as her daughter filed the last nail and applied the base coat.

"I filed an application with the university the other day. Yes, I'm tired of my children being worried—well one of them anyway—and I think I'm ready to move on to another chapter in my life. I can teach meteorology instead of flying into the middle of it. And I have a wealth of experience to bring to the job." Sandy put the final touches of pale pink on her mother's toenails, placed her flip flops on her feet and moved the pan of water. "Can you walk? Cause I think the dough should be about ready."

The warm crisp cookie crumbled onto the plate as Billie sipped the iced tea. "These are wonderful, Martha. And I can't believe they came out this well with me baking them."

"You did a great job. My mother's Snickerdoodle recipe is wonderful, but remember to refrigerate the dough and bake them no longer than eight minutes. That's the key. And I think the dough is even better if it is refrigerated overnight." Martha dried the big blue bowl as Sandy washed the last of the dishes.

"Giselle likes shrimp, doesn't she?" Sandy looked at her friend sitting at the table breaking another cookie apart.

"Yes."

"Why don't we go down to the dock and get some shrimp for tonight. We could cook at your house, Billie. And Giselle and Raven could eat too." Sandy looked at her mother and her friend.

"Oh, my mother would love that." Billie stood putting the last of the cookies in the plastic container.

"Okay, Mom, get the shrimp pot out; we're taking the feast on the road."

Chapter 19

At the dock, you could easily pick out the shrimper alongside the yachts. Paul's shrimp boat was not only twice as big, but much older, a workhorse, not built for pleasure. The seagulls screeched overhead as the men brought the boat into the harbor, dinner time for the birds as well as the customers.

"What are a couple of pretty ladies like you doing on the dock this evening?" Paul's deeply tanned face still smiled even after a hard day of shrimping. He loved his job.

"We're looking for shrimp. You got any?" Sandy stepped on board the boat and gave her uncle a hug.

"Only the best shrimp on the coast. Whatcha got to trade?" Paul eyed his niece.

"Money?"

"Oh, your money's no good here. Meg just brought me some blackberries." Paul held up a basket of fresh berries dotted with dew and glistening in the sun.

"Well, we have some fresh Snickerdoodles back at the house. I could go get you some." Billie smiled.

"If you didn't bring them with you, what good does that do me? How many pounds do you want?"

"Two should be plenty. We're having a shrimp boil tonight at Billie's. Come on by or are you tired of shrimp?" Sandy took the package of shrimp from the deckhand.

"Never tired of shrimp. This guy isn't either." Paul pointed to the man who stood behind Billie.

"Hi, Neil. I didn't see you there." Billie felt a blush again.

"The shrimp boats are a popular place this time of evening." He smiled. "One pound please." He handed over the money to the deckhand.

"Sandy is fixing shrimp boil tonight with our moms." Billie had no idea why she had to explain herself.

"Sounds good. Mike and I are cooking some on the boat. When are you coming by to see her?" Neil pushed the hat back on his head. "She's right over there." He pointed down the dock.

"Go ahead, hon, I'm going to talk to Uncle Paul for a minute." Sandy stepped back as the water rushed across the deck. Deckhands tossed buckets of sea water to rinse the residue from the catch back into the ocean. Sea gulls dove to pick up the scraps screeching loudly at their neighbors.

Billie paused and then wondered why she felt so shy. Neil, a nice man, had a nice boat. What was the harm in it?

"Sure." She brushed the hair out of her face and Neil gestured toward the boat with *Overboard* painted on the stern.

Billie sat on the seat with a bottle of water chatting when Sandy arrived with the bag of fresh shrimp, gulls following her.

"Are you busy tomorrow?" Billie looked at her friend. "Want to take a boat ride?"

****

The shrimp pot, set up in the front yard of sand and

sea grass, began to boil the salted water. A small bundle of spices wrapped in cheese cloth floated on the surface leaking out its precious flavor to be soaked up by the prawns and vegetables. Billie dumped the potatoes and corn into the water, allowing them to cook a little before the shellfish went in. She leaned over the pot and breathed in the succulent smell.

Giselle sat in her chair on the porch as the sun set behind fluffy white clouds. A light breeze blew her gray hair away from her face and she closed her eyes serenely. "This is lovely, ladies." Giselle spoke for the first time since pushed out onto the porch. "We need to do this more often. It's not that Raven's cooking isn't wonderful, but a shrimp boil on the beach is hard to beat."

Raven walked out the front door with a tray of glasses and two frosty bottles. "Ladies, I have wine to go with the fish tonight. A light chardonnay or a light bubbly non-alcoholic chardonnay—or some kind of grape juice." She pointed to the bottles then poured them into glasses and handed them around.

Billie sat on the swing as Sandy dumped the shrimp into the water. "A toast is in order, I think. To my five favorite women in the world and the shrimp that gave up their lives to feed us."

"Whether they wanted to or not." Sandy giggled and raised her glass.

Giselle sipped the bubbly grape juice and let it roll down her throat. Her hand began to shake, and she placed it on the tray balanced on the arms of the chair. "I don't think I've eaten mashed shrimp boil before, but there is always a first time for everything."

"How long before the shrimp is ready? I'll get the

garlic rolls." Raven stepped back into the house.

Giselle scooped tiny morsels of chopped and mashed shrimp, corn and potatoes and pulled small pieces off the soft garlic rolls, munching happily with her friends and family. She rinsed it down with sips of bubbly juice. She had not eaten this much food for a while. Raven perched next to her charge helping her when she needed it.

Sandy and Billie sat together on the swing like they did when they were children, and Martha took the folding chair close by. The small screened in porch, full to capacity with shrimp eaters, began to cool in the evening breeze.

"I forgot, Martha and I made cookies today. Dessert anyone?" Billie got up to go to the kitchen listening to the groans behind her.

"Sweetie, could I get a cup of tea to go with them?" Giselle asked as her daughter walked in the house.

"One pot of tea coming up," she replied.

Chapter 20

Sandy looked into the distance, still surprised that she and Billie were on the boat with the guys. They seemed to be nice people, but she never thought Billie would go on anything resembling a date.

By habit she watched the weather; the lightning in the distance caught her eye. No one else noticed. Neil played guitar again, poorly. Mike followed her around most of the time, even on the small boat. The boat itself wasn't that small, forty feet, but with four people occupying space, it shrank. Four people each had ten feet to call their own—that is if they lay end to end on the top—and they wouldn't do that. Inside, it felt smaller.

But Billie laughed at all of Neil's jokes—something she didn't do much anymore. No matter how much she saw her therapist and took the meds assigned to help her, she wouldn't be the same person Sandy grew up with. But maybe that was okay.

Billie had agreed to go out with the men on the boat, and Sandy intended to see to it she had a good time. She put her feet up on the seat and looked out to sea.

They had drifted out beyond sight of land. Sandy wondered if anyone else noticed that. They were too busy having fun, and that got boaters into trouble. The squall she saw in the distance seemed a long way off, but squalls moved fast. It might take a while to reach shore. They needed to head for home

"Guys, there's a squall to the south and we need to be heading back in." Neil continued to play—or pick out tunes. Whatever he did with the guitar did not include piloting the ship. "Neil," Sandy continued. He looked up. "There's a storm headed our way. We need to be getting back."

"Where?" He shaded his eyes and looked toward land.

Sandy pointed behind him. "To the south. The harbor is the opposite way." She pointed.

"Are you sure?" Neil got up, setting the guitar to the side. He walked to the control station and tapped on the compass. Why did men do that, Sandy wondered. Magnetic north was magnetic north. Tapping didn't change things.

Lightning flashed again, closer this time. "And it's headed this way." Sandy held her hand up to shade her eyes and looked out to sea. The dark blue water and sunlight above belied the weather in the distance where the sky was darker.

"Well, it's a long way off." Neil started to pick up the instrument again.

"We need to go." Billie's smile had disappeared.

"Now? We were just having fun." Neil strummed.

"Now, captain." Sandy reached for the guitar.

"Please." Billie began to shake, and Sandy knew how quickly things could get bad with her. "Let's get in before it hits."

Neil stared at the damaged woman.

"Come on, bud, let's get the ladies in before they get wet." Mike patted his friend on the shoulder as

Sandy took the guitar and headed for the galley.

They needed to clear off the deck in case they couldn't outrun the storm. When she turned around, Mike had toted the ice chest down the stairs with Billie right behind him carrying the picnic lunch. Sandy heard the engine start up and felt the boat turn around, headed the other way. At least Neil knew how to use a compass. Nice as he was, he needed work on his piloting skills. An unseasoned captain on a stormy sea could spell disaster.

Billie walked past her on the way to the berth after she put the lunch in the tiny refrigerator. Sandy could hear her rummaging through closets and drawers.

"Where are the life jackets?" Her voice went up several notes when stressed.

"Try the drawers under the bed, sweetie."

Sandy hoped they would not be needed, but if it helped Billie feel more secure, then she should have one.

"Found 'em." Billie came out with her life jacket secured around her and three others in her hands. She gave one to Sandy who quickly put it on, smelling the musty odor of a seldom used vest. Once wet, it didn't smell new. She knew it had been stowed away without a thorough drying.

Once on top, Sandy found the men tending to the boat, and the sky darkening behind them. Billie handed the life jackets to Neil and Mike. Neil promptly dropped his at his feet as he piloted the boat. She didn't know where Mike's went.

"Is this as fast as she'll go?" Billie slid up next to Sandy and placed her hand up to shade her eyes looking toward land.

Mike smiled at Billie with what looked like indulgence. "Hey captain—can this bucket of bolts move any faster?"

Neil turned and gave his friend a look of disdain then glanced at Billie. "Everybody have a seat. We're going to find out how this baby handles the waves," he said as he pushed the throttle forward.

The boat lurched throwing Billie backward, she grabbed Sandy's arm. They sat down together on the bench and looked out to sea. The squall gave the boat a run for its money as the dark sky in the south moved toward them like a shroud.

Winds shifted and began to blow from the east, pushing the small boat away from its intended target. Sandy immediately noticed the change.

"Neil," she stood and walked his way. "That wind has changed. What's the compass look like?" She watched in amazement when he tapped it with his finger then looked into the distance. The waves threatened to knock her off her feet, and she grabbed the back of his chair just as she caught site of the rocky shore just for a second. Then it disappeared again.

"There it is." Sandy pointed toward the land.

"There what is?" He looked back down at his instruments and reached for the compass again.

"Land. I saw it for a second. You know tapping that thing makes no difference, right?" Sandy glanced back at her friend who sat motionless and stared toward the shore.

"I didn't see it. I think this east wind is blowing us off course." Neil looked again in the wrong direction.

"It's right there, see the dot to the right a little? That's the rocky shore, on the far end of the island."

Sandy stood pointing to land with her finger.

"Yes, I sometimes fish off those rocks." Neil adjusted the nose of the ship toward the rocks. "Thanks, I didn't see them."

"Well, I lived on the island a long time and know how the winds normally blow around here." Sandy smiled and touched his shoulder when the crack of lightning flashed beside them. She glanced at Billie sitting straight up and looking at the shore. Then the rains came down in sheets.

"Billie, hon, why don't you and Mike get below where it's dry?" Sandy tried to sound calm but knew things weren't good as the small boat tossed and turned. "Billie?" She looked around to see her friend frozen.

"Mike, can you help her out?" Sandy nodded to her friend, and Mike quickly took the bait, helping Billie to her feet and into the hull of the boat. Sandy would remain with the captain to assist with getting them into shore in one piece.

The increased speed of the boat helped to take the waves, as the boat sometimes sliced across the top of them, then down into their depths. Still the boat rocked from side to side making little headway. Neil kept an eye on the compass and headed for the rocks that showed up on the opposite end of the island from where he tied the boat.

"Once we get closer to the rocks we can head into the wind and should be able to make the harbor. Just keep the rocks in sight." Neil nodded. He was an amateur. Thankfully Sandy wasn't. A gust of wind sucked the hat off his head and blew it into the darkened sky just as a rogue wave ran up and over the boat soaking Sandy and Neil to the bone. He wiped the water from his eyes but never took them off the intended target. He might have been lax about leaving when he should, but he remained vigilant about getting them home.

The engine churned, pushing the boat against the angry sea. Sandy hung onto the back of Neil's chair losing her balance several times on the wet and slippery deck. She could not stay dry with the rain and the waves flowing over the hull. Suddenly the wind shifted again, this time to the rear of the boat. It blew them toward the rocks and the island at a faster rate of speed. At this rate, they would make shore in a hurry.

"Well, that helped." Neil looked up at his co-pilot as the boat picked up speed toward the shore.

Sandy spoke with authority. "It will get us there quickly. When I tell you, you need to turn this thing around and push it toward the harbor. We can't afford to hit those rocks. It will push us right into them, if we let it." Neil didn't hesitate. The boat picked up speed— either headed for safety or destruction on the rocks.

"Okay now, turn the craft toward the west end of the island. We'll have to crab into the wind some, because it will try to push us into the island too quickly or turn us over. Do you want to do this or me?" Sandy didn't want to sound bossy, but she knew the sea better than Neil.

"No, I've got it. Here we go." Neil turned the rudder, and the boat crabbed into the wind at an angle, the waves threatening to roll them over as he turned sideways to them. The next wave swamped the boat. Sandy found herself thrown sideways smacking her head on the wall. She held on to the secured captain's chair for her life. If she went overboard, she would never see land again. She watched as the life jacket thrown at Neil's feet earlier washed overboard. She couldn't afford to retrieve it. The waves were relentless, pushing the boat sideways, closer to the island.

Slowly the boat made headway to the other part of the island where the marina sat—and the sudden squall began to blow away. The small storm rushed toward the mainland. The boat moved the opposite way from the storm as the weather raced on to batter the coast line before falling apart over land. Soon the lights of the harbor could be seen in the distance, and the sun peeked out from dark clouds only to be covered up again-soon to reemerge completely. "There it is." Neil breathed a sigh of relief.

Sandy brushed wet hair from her eyes and patted Neil on the arm. "I don't mean to be rude, Neil, but you've got to watch the weather when you're on the ocean. It can take you out in a second." Sandy nodded to the man who captained his own boat into harm's way. He nodded back like a little boy.

Soaked, Sandy went below to check on her friend as Neil expertly pulled into his slip at the marina. She found Billie sitting rigidly on the twin bed with Mike beside her. Billie didn't need any more trauma in her life. By the time they reached the harbor, the storm was a memory—at least on Sandhill Island.

Once at the slip, Poppy walked their direction to help tie up the vessel. He probably hoped Neil would tip him. He often made some pocket change that way.

"You guys are all wet. Did the storm getcha?" Poppy held his hand out to Billie as she stepped up on the dock.

"Not quite, but it tried," she replied, and Sandy

took her arm as they headed for home. Neil had a lot to learn about the ocean.

Chapter 21

With her arm around the shoulders of the oldest friend Sandy had ever had, she walked with Billie back to the house from the dock. Neil tried to explain, but Sandy said Billie, distraught, needed to lie down. They would talk later. The friends didn't talk on the way home. Sandy knew Billie needed her space.

Drenched, they walked in the door of the house Billie and her mother lived in most of their lives. Raven carried a basket of laundry into the living room, then she immediately stopped what she was doing and ran to Billie's side.

"Honey, are you okay? What happened?" Raven wrapped Billie in the cocoon of an afghan and handed a large bath towel to Sandy.

"There was a storm." Sandy wiped her face with the towel.

"I can see that. I'm making tea," Raven announced quietly and turned toward the kitchen.

Giselle was still taking her afternoon nap, and Billie didn't want to disturb her.

Raven returned quickly with two steaming mugs. "The kettle was already hot. Okay, so what happened? It barely rained here on the island. This," she gestured to the two women in front of her, "must have happened out on the open water."

"We ran into a squall. It caught us off guard."

Sandy toweled her long blond hair dry.

"Caught you off guard? You? Try again." Raven looked at Sandy like her mother when as a child she lied.

"Okay, it caught the captain off guard. I tried to tell him, but you know how men are. Anyway, it was a fast mover, and I think it would have caught up with us even if he had moved when I suggested."

Billie stared off into space wrapped in the throw. Then she lifted her head and began to speak.

"The storm caught us by surprise. But what really caught me by surprise was my reaction. It's not like I've never been in a storm or soaked to the bone before. So, what is my problem?" She wiped away a tear and then sobbed into the arms of her mother's nurse.

"Your problem is you are still delicate. Too much too soon." Raven smoothed her dark wet hair with a second towel.

"So, when will I be normal again? We ran into a little storm, and I froze like a statue. The car wreck happened two years ago and had nothing to do with storms, or boats, or anything." She reached for a tissue on the coffee table, blew her nose and took the steaming mug of tea that sat on the coffee table. It took both hands to hold it steady.

"Your doctor would say 'what's normal?' And she would be right. What is normal for one is not normal for the next." Raven handed a second cup to Sandy.

"Raven?" A weak voice called from Giselle's bedroom. The aging woman had finished her nap.

"Be right there," Raven called back over her shoulder.

"I don't want her to see me like this. I'm going to

change." Billie walked toward her own bedroom while Raven took care of her patient.

Knocking on the bedroom door, Sandy entered to find her friend toweling her hair dry. She stared into the mirror that hung above the dresser. The afghan laid on the bed. Sandy picked it up and draped it over the rocker that sat in the corner to dry, then hung her own towel on a hook.

"I'm so tired of being a mess." Billie spoke to the mirror as much as her friend. She leaned in and looked at her eyes, wiping one with the towel.

"I don't think you're a mess. I think you just still need time." Sandy patted her friend's shoulder then gave it a little squeeze. "I'm going to go home before your Mom gets up. You and I will talk later, okay? You did fine out there today. It was a storm on the water. They're scary to everyone. I want you to remember that. We were all scared, even if we didn't want to admit it. And you did fine." She quickly hugged her friend and left the bedroom, closing the door behind her, then walked out the front door of the small house and down the road toward her mother's home. She and Billie would talk again later. Maybe she'd join her for Yoga early in the morning.

****

Billie's long dark hair swayed in the breeze as she sat cross-legged on the mat. Seagulls screeched overhead, always on the lookout for a morsel. Waves rolled rhythmically in as the sea breeze blew, and the sun moved higher into the sky.

"You just going to stand there or are you going to speak?" Billie smiled when she turned around to see Sandy standing behind her.

"I didn't want to interrupt. I see you found some sea glass." Sandy knelt next to the stacked stones and picked up the tiny pieces of sanded glass the ocean offered up from a treasure trove that lay beneath her waves. They were frosted from the tumbling they took as they rolled over sand and were smoothed to perfection. She held it up to the sun to look through its icy aqua blue color and wondered what it once had been. A bottle? Bowl? Only the sea knew, and she wasn't talking.

"Pretty, isn't it? We have a jar in the kitchen and I add to it now and then. There is a woman in town that makes jewelry from it, and I give her what I find."

"Lovely." Sandy put the colored glass back on the sand and stood. "How are you this morning?"

"I feel a little like the sea glass—tumbled relentlessly." Billie stood from her mat and turned to face her friend.

"Well, a little sanding off the rough edges could do us all some good."

"At this rate, I'll be smooth as silk soon." Billie smiled and brushed back the hair from her face.

"I'm going home today. The kids are due back tomorrow. Then I am going to start the paperwork to resign my commission. I got the job offer from the school, and I start classes in September."

"Oh, that's wonderful! I'm so happy for you, Sandy. If anyone deserves this, it is you. You've worked so hard."

"Well, I'm ready. I'll tell the kids when I get home and then we'll be back soon. I want to spend as much time as possible with you and Mom this summer between jobs. Then I'll be rested and relaxed when the new job starts in the fall." Sandy stirred the colored glass with one toe.

"By the way, did you call your doctor about the incident yesterday?" Sandy looked up from the sand.

"No. I hate to go running to her every time I have a little glitch. When will it end? I need to learn to handle a few things myself." Billie rolled the Yoga mat up and stuffed it in the bag.

"True, you do. But don't wait too long if the symptoms return." Sandy leaned in and hugged her friend. "I'll let you know when I get home; and when I have a date to be back, I'll let you know that too."

"Oh, and by the way, there is paint left over. Maybe we should think about painting your house when I get back. That is if you like yellow and white. I'm never good at knowing how much to buy, so I buy too much. You take care of yourself. Tell Giselle and Raven bye for me, and I'll see you soon." Sandy waved goodbye as she walked away.

Billie wiped a tear away. She was crying again.

Chapter 22

The blustery wind shook salt water from the screens of her mother's beach house windows. The morning had started off cool and rainy, but the rain had quickly subsided.

"Take a jacket," Sandy called to her children after the battle to get them out of shorts and into jeans. Still wearing flip flops, they ran out the door for the opposite end of the island, happy to be out of the house. Mom finally trusted them out alone on Grandma's island. They were going to be here for a few weeks this time.

Barely away from the house, Jake turned. "Why are you following me?"

Carol stopped short of running into him.

"Where am I supposed to go?" Carol's eyes showed the pain of his remark.

"Huuuhh." The air blew out between Jake's clenched teeth. "Anywhere but here! Go do something. I don't need a baby sister following me everywhere I go." He stomped off toward the opposite end of the island unzipping his jacket leaving it flying open in the wind, never looking back.

Carol stood still and watched him go, then crouched down to pick up the tiny sea shells in the road. She looked them over in her palm and pocketed the ones she found the most interesting, then continued to walk.

Brothers! Who needed them anyway? She knew this island as well as he did, and she could find her way alone. He forgot he was only one year older than her. She'd been around a while too, and knew Grandma's island as well as anyone. Mom told them to stay together, but as usual, Jake didn't listen. She'd just let him go, and then he'd be the one that got in trouble, not her.

Unconsciously she continued to follow Jake. At least she walked the same way he did—toward the rocks. Carol knew Mom didn't like her near them, which made them more attractive. When she saw Jake climbing up and over, she stopped and shook her head. She turned toward Le Chez. Maybe Sam would give her some of his wonderful rolls if she looked especially pitiful.

She walked idly toward the restaurant. Someone she didn't recognize swept the deck where Aunt Billie sang. Carol wished she could sing as well as Billie, and she'd leave her brother and never look back. Of course, she'd have to get Mom's permission, but once an adult, she'd never have to see her brother again.

Sam stepped out the side door of the restaurant with a pan in his hands. Lillie appeared instantly at his side. Billie's new dog, Lillie, kept getting fatter and maybe Carol knew why. She ate Sam's food and Billie's. Sam bent down and scooped the scraps into a bowl for Lillie, and then picked up the water bowl, dumping it on the ground.

"Hi Sam," Carol spoke shyly.

Sam looked up from petting the long brown dog. "Hi Carol. Are you alone? Where's your mother?"

Carol reached down to pet Lillie. "She's at

Grandma's. Jake and I were supposed to be out together, but he ran off. I think he's on the rocks, and he'll get in trouble when Mom finds out."

Sam looked toward the rocks. "Well, it's just too bad that he'll miss the rolls I've been baking. They're hot out of the oven. Want some?"

Carol's eyes flew open wide and she looked up no longer shy. "Yes! And can Lillie have one too?"

"Well, we'll see if there are any leftover from yesterday for Lillie. I need to keep a few for the customers." Sam filled Lillie's water bowl and then opened the door for Carol.

The inside of the restaurant smelled like her grandmother's kitchen. Always something cooking. Maybe Carol would like to be a chef like Sam instead of a singer like Billie, then she could have all the rolls she wanted.

Sam led her to a table and pulled a chair out for her. He returned from the kitchen with a tray holding a basket of rolls, two plates, a container of butter, and two glasses of tea.

"Help yourself, little lady. Your brother will be sad he missed this." Sam smiled and buttered a roll.

Carol smeared butter on the roll she took from the basket and licked the excess off her fingers. She took a bite of the warm bread dripping in butter, and it melted in her mouth. Then she ate another. She ate until stuffed while Sam chatted asking about school and what she wanted to do when she grew up.

"I thought I wanted to be a singer like Billie, but now I might want to be a chef like you. Could you teach me to make rolls?"

"You bet. Oh, I have a customer. You eat all you

want. Your mother will hang me for spoiling your dinner." Sam smiled then walked away toward the man and woman who stepped in the door. Sam treated everyone nicely.

Finally, Carol pushed the plate away, she couldn't eat another bite. She took the last roll and wrapped it in a paper napkin. She'd give it to Lillie. After all, Sam said she could have all she wanted. And she walked toward the exit.

"Thank you, Sam," she said as she waved and left through the front door. Walking to the side of the building, she looked for the dog. She was nowhere to be found. And then she headed back to the rocks. She'd tell Jake about the rolls and how he missed out.

Jake's jacket lay crumpled where she'd last seen him climbing the rocks. But she didn't see Jake. She shoved the roll in her sweatshirt pocket and then took it off. She dropped the sweatshirt on the ground next to Jake's.

She turned to the panting as Lillie ran up behind her. The long brown nose searched the sweatshirt for the bread she smelled.

"Hi, Lillie. I brought you something." Carol reached in the pocket and pulled out the smashed roll wrapped in a napkin. Pulling off a small piece, she fed it to the anxious dog.

"Lillie, you are getting fat! Mom says you're having puppies." Carol giggled at the dog who nosed her hand for more. "You want some more? Huh? More roll?" She giggled louder as the dog jumped for her hand and then let out a happy yelp.

"I've never heard you bark. Good girl." Carol ran her hand over the velvet pelt of the dog feeling the wiggling puppies inside. She wondered if Mom would let her have one of the puppies. Of course, it would be a while before it could leave its mother. But they were planning to spend the summer here. Maybe before they left the island to go back to school the puppies would be old enough. She fed the pregnant dog another piece of the roll and fell into laughter as the dog grabbed the bread.

"Carol!" A voice on the other side of the rocks called. It sounded like Jake, but Carol knew Jake would not call his baby sister no matter what.

"Carol! Are you there? I need help!" The voice did belong to Jake—and came from the other side of the rocks.

Running to the rocks with the dog right behind her she climbed to the top and looked down. Jake stood in water up to his knees.

"You're gonna be in trouble. Mom said not to get wet."

"I'm stuck! I can't get out!" Jake retorted, showing her his legs.

"How did you do that?" Carol slid down the giant boulder toward her brother.

"Carol, wait! Don't come any closer. You'll get stuck too."

"Well, how did you do that, silly?" Carol reached for his hand.

"I just stepped into this hole to get the starfish and my pant leg got stuck. Now the tide's coming in." On cue, a wave rushed over the children soaking both to the bone.

"Augh, I'm wet. Mom's gonna kill me!" Carol looked up at Lillie barking above her. It was a frantic sound. "Here, take my hand, and I'll pull you free." Carol reached for Jake and his outstretched hand. She pulled, but her hand slipped free as another wave crashed over them both.

"I tried to push the rock back, but my jeans are stuck. I can't get my pants out. See?" Jake pushed on the rock that held his pants. Carol reached down into the water and pulled on his leg and realized the water now reached his thighs. The tide rose, and Jake might not have much time.

"Take 'em off," she cried as she looked at his soaked jeans.

"I can't take off my pants. How would I get home?"

"You have to; the water is getting deeper. You'll drown!" The waves crashed again soaking them both as Lillie barked above.

Jake looked pleadingly at his sister. "Turn around," he commanded as another wave washed over both of them. Carol turned her head and then heard a splash that didn't sound like a wave. Jake shimmied out of his jeans and fell backwards in the process. He floated in the ocean. She reached out grabbing his hand and pulling him toward the shore. They scrambled up on the wet slippery rocks as the dog continued to bark. Carol turned and looked down at the floating jeans. Mom would kill Jake.

Without thinking she went back for the clothes stuck between the rocks and floating in the water. She grabbed them and pulled just as the wave crashed over her head sucking her off the rocks and into the pool. She held on to the pants for her life to keep from being washed out to sea. Salt water up her nose and in her mouth, she coughed as she used the wedged jeans to pull herself hand over hand back onto the rocks. Then another wave, and this time the strength of the water moved the rock just enough.

They were free!

She held the pants with one hand and the rock with the other. The next thing she knew Jake was pulling her to safety. They both climbed higher up the rocks with the water rising behind them.

At the top, she realized she still had Jake's jeans in her hands. She handed them to her brother and once again turned around, so he could dress. Lillie stood sentry at the top. As Carol climbed over the top of the rocky shore, Lillie licked her face. Dripping, Carol reached down for her sweatshirt.

"You saved my life." Jake stared at his baby sister in astonishment.

"You were drowning," she said matter-of-factly. "And Mom would kill you if you lost your pants."

Jake helped her into her sweatshirt reaching around her shoulders. He almost hugged her as he did.

"I can't believe you saved me and then went back for my jeans. For a little sister, you're all right." Jake smiled at his sister for the first time in a long time.

"That's okay; you'd do it for me," Carol replied. "What are we gonna tell Mom?" Carol asked as they walked back toward the beach house. They both imagined a conversation with Mom they didn't want to have.

"I'll say I fell in trying to get a starfish, and you helped me back up." He smiled again and pushed her wet hair out of her face.

Maybe brothers were okay after all. "You missed

the fresh rolls at Le Chez." Carol rubbed Lillie's head as they walked home together.

Chapter 23

Billie sang most of the set solo that evening as the tourists ate shrimp and fish until they could eat no more. String had a summer cold. His throat raspy, she tried to give him a break.

"You sound like Dr. John," she said giving his shoulder a shove.

"Maybe that's not a bad thing." String laughed which caused another coughing fit. "But I don't want to infect the microphone or anyone that uses it. Would you be opposed to quitting early? The last group is about to pass out anyway. Sam will send them home soon. I think I may have Mitch, the bartender, give me a walking hot toddy and go to bed early."

"Mitch is the best. I'll bet he has something in mind that might help you. And since you're just sleeping upstairs, I think a to-go cup would be allowed. A hot toddy sounds good. I wish I could have a drink now and then. I look forward to the day I am off the meds and back on my feet—and not just for a drink." Billie closed down the piano and stowed the cords after she signaled to Sam. He normally checked the deck around this time of night to be sure the customers were taken care of. The kitchen was done for the evening.

The last diner walked in and sat in the back. She squinted trying to see in the mist that blew up from the sea. She thought it was Neil. He sat with a drink in his hand and waited until the waiter brought his dinner in a bag.

Billie felt badly that she hadn't seen him much lately. Since the day of the squall he had not come around. Maybe she needed to talk to him.

Leaving the stage in the hands of String and the busboys, she walked toward Neil's table.

"I haven't seen you in a while." Billie smiled at the man standing to leave after he gave the waiter a tip.

"Hey, it's good to see you. I wasn't sure you wanted me around after the storm." Neil looked apprehensive. "You know your friend was right. I need to learn about the weather around here. In fact, I talked to Paul about going out on the shrimper with him a little. I know he knows things you can't find in books."

"That's true. Anyway, it's okay. Everyone's got to learn. I know nothing about ice and snow in Montana." A moth circled around the light on the deck and flew between them.

"Well, I could tell you all about it, but I really don't want to go back and live there again. I think I'm sticking around for a while."

"Good. That's good to hear." Billie, glad he had decided to stick around, felt badly about how she last left him.

"It is good to know you're not permanently traumatized. I hated how you left the boat that day." Neil batted at the moth.

"I'm fine, really. I should have contacted you before now. I told Sandy, I'm tired of being scared or upset all the time." Billie tucked her hair behind one ear.

"You had a right to be scared that day. I think we

all were. But as long as you are okay."

"I'm fine." String tapped her on the shoulder and nodded upstairs. "Good night, String, take care." He walked away with a glass in his hand.

"Maybe a drink some evening after your set?" Neil looked apprehensive again.

"I don't drink—meds you know."

"Well, it doesn't have to be alcohol. Anything you want."

"That would be nice. Some other time? String has a summer cold and is going to bed with a night- cap. He probably needs it. And I think I'll take off too. It was good to see you." She nodded goodbye as she walked away toward the kitchen.

Chapter 24

The fog horn sounded for anyone crazy enough to be out to sea that night. Joe Franks walked through the darkened neighborhood aware only of the sounds of the surf. His eyes had adjusted to the darkness. The island shut down at night. The few streetlights were shrouded in mist and fog. The breeze blew mounds of grounded clouds away only to be replaced by another.

Franks thought she would be home now. He saw the restaurant close the deck when the fog rolled in, and he assumed she went home early. He'd roamed this island enough to decide which house she lived in, one of the many in need of paint. The same one the mongrel dog frequented. She probably fed it. He wondered if she knew it would soon present her with other mouths to feed.

He saw a light on in the back of the house, but he could see no movement. He heard the backdoor slam and slid around the corner to see who walked out. Creeping under the window on one side of the house, he edged up over the sill and peeked. In the dark room, he could make out a bed in the middle of the room. A chair sat next to the bed—probably the old woman's wheelchair. Surely, she slept.

Sneaking along the rough wooden siding, he reached the corner of the house where the noise came from. A figure bent over trash cans filling them for the next collection. When she raised her head, he recognized the dark face of the nurse. Billie must be in the house. A good time to talk to her with the nurse out of the picture and Mom in bed. A red dot formed in the center of the woman's face, and Franks smelled the acrid smoke of cigarettes. The nurse walked out for a smoke break. That gave him even more time.

Walking hunched over along the side of the house to the front screened door, he heard panting underfoot. The dog. It lay under the porch, but it made no move to stop him or alert those in the house of his intent. The pant became a whine, but evidently the dog felt no need to warn the woman who fed her. He stopped and slowly took a step onto the front porch. The door of the house stood just a few feet away. Reaching up, he turned the knob, knowing no one locked their doors on Sandhill Island, and stepped into the house.

The light was on in the kitchen at the back; he slowly made his way through the house looking for the woman who ruined his life. He might have to scare her this time to make her realize he meant business. No one occupied the kitchen. Maybe she had already gone to bed. He opened the door of the bedroom next to the kitchen and walked blindly to the bed. The fog blew away enough to shine a moment of moonlight into the room, enough for Franks to see an unoccupied bed. The nurse was out back. If Billie wasn't home, that meant the only other person in the house had to be the old lady. Maybe he should pay her a visit. Scare the old woman enough, and she would surely tell Billie. She might be of some use after all.

He crept to the open door of the second bedroom and saw a lump in the middle of the bed. He'd heard she had Parkinson's, a disease that led to the failure of her legs—so she had a wheelchair. She wouldn't be able to run very far.

At the edge of the bed, he could hear the soft breathing and smell the stink of old woman. Old age and sickness ravaged her body. He leaned over her, and she suddenly jumped, letting out a small screech. Franks quickly put his grimy hand over her face and nose. He hoped the nurse remained outside enjoying her cigarette.

"Don't move and don't make a sound." He pressed down harder to let her know he meant business. She struggled slightly, and he pushed harder.

"I said be still! Where's Billie? Where's your daughter?" He released his hold, so she could answer.

She gasped, and her body shook. "Who—who are you?" She spoke with all the urgency her frail body could muster.

"I said, where's Billie? Don't mess with me old woman. I know you're sick, but you still know where your daughter is."

"At work." She gasped as she talked, and trembled under his touch—one hand still on her neck.

"She left hours ago; the fog rolled in and they shut down the deck."

"Then I don't know. I'm sure she'll be home soon. Please, go away." The old woman's trembling increased.

Franks leaned in close to the woman's gasping lips. "You tell her I'm tired of asking. You tell Billie that the time has come for her to help me out. I need another job, and she is going to help me get it. It's her fault I had to go to jail and lost every penny I ever had. Now it is time for her to pay up." Giselle squirmed under his hand and tried to get away by shoving his face with her hands and scooting backwards on useless legs. She swung her arm up pushing herself away from him and slipped off the backside of the small bed. Her movements knocked over the antique glass lamp, shattering it on the hardwood floor. Giselle let out a weak scream followed by a moan. She must have been cut from the glass. And the fall would do her no good either.

The dog under the porch suddenly howled in alarm and the backdoor slammed. Franks ran for the front of the house, out the door and across the porch. He heard the nurse behind him screaming at him to stop. Keeping his stride, he ran into the foggy night.

****

Crooning into the microphone, Billie felt a change in the temperature and the sea breeze became clammier than normal, her dress clinging to bare legs. Fog rolled in off the ocean and up across the island like a sticky, translucent, marshmallow cream. She glanced off the deck and knew the low-lying clouds would quickly cover the island in a thick blanket. She nodded to String. Both of them had lived near the water long enough to know the signs. Sea fog, not like the kind that lived in the ditches on land, had a mind of its own—it came and went uninvited, and would stay as long as it liked.

She signaled String to take a break and walked toward the door of the restaurant. She would get some help to move the equipment inside. Patrons would be leaving soon. She waved at Neil as she walked by his table near the back of the deck. Lately he sat at the same table on the weekends, and she knew the reason. He came to see her.

The large double doors quickly opened, and bus boys arrived to move her precious piano back inside in the corner and out of the weather. There were few diners left, inside or out, and many were leaving because of the fog.

She helped String and the bus boys with the rest of the equipment, stacking it under the piano and out of the way. They were done for the evening.

"Well, that was fast. I didn't hear about fog in the forecast for this evening." Billie spoke to String or anyone standing near.

"We might as well call it a night. There's hardly anyone left anyway." String placed the amp under the piano with the cords stacked on top.

"Can I take you home?" Billie turned to find Neil behind her. "My car is outside, and you might get lost out there and end up in the water."

The restaurant cleared out, the last of the customers stood in line paying their bills. Sam would lose money tonight due to the weather.

Billie hesitated. She needed to let Neil back in her life. After all, the storm on the ocean that day wasn't his fault. She knew it wasn't safe to be walking; she might get hit by a car. Maybe she should accept the offer. "That would be nice, thank you."

Neil broke into the biggest smile she had ever seen on his face. "Do we have time for a drink before we leave?"

"Take your time," Sam said as he silently appeared beside her. "We'll clean up around you. And thanks for taking our girl home. It's good to know she will be in good hands. My place is just out the back door and String stays upstairs on the weekends. Billie lives the farthest away."

"Thank you. I'll have a club soda." Billie sat at the one table that did not have the chairs already stacked on it.

"Make that two," Neil said to the waiter who probably had other duties to attend to.

"I can't stay long. Mom is already in bed and Raven is probably tired. She has a bed at our house and sleeps there when I work, but it is nice to have her around. Mom's not getting better and sometimes it takes both of us. I don't know what I'd do without her."

Sam arrived with the drinks, his waiters and bus boys scrambling around him. When Neil tried to pay, Sam waved him away, then walked to the back.

"So, how long does this fog last?" Neil took a long draw from the drink.

"It lasts as long as it wants but normally all night and into the morning. The sun will burn it off unless the wind comes up and blows it away during the night. That's just part of the charm of living on an island."

"And you wouldn't live anywhere else?" Neil looked Billie up and down

"I don't think so. I really love it here. I go into Corpus when I have to, but this place is just right for me. And as long as Mom needs me, I'm not going anywhere. I know she won't be around forever."

"Well, it is beautiful, and I love the warm weather. I've lived in Montana most of my life, but hated the cold. I don't know what took me so long to leave. In fact, maybe I won't go back. I've thought of branching out and setting up a business here, too. My buddy in

Montana could run the one up there and I could run the one here. I don't know, just a thought."

Billie drained her glass. Singing made her thirsty. The water bottle on the piano was long gone.

"Are you ready to go?" Neil took another sip. "I just want to say how nice it is just sitting here talking and getting to know another human being. Especially a beautiful one."

Billie felt herself blush in the darkening restaurant.

"Yes, I need to get going." She picked up the glasses and took them to the kitchen where she stored her purse, then walked back to the man who had offered her a ride home.

Neil opened the door and was greeted by a scene out of a Stephen King movie. "It's like looking through waxed paper. I'm not sure my mom's pea soup was this thick," he said as he led her to the car by the building. Opening the door for her, he walked around to the driver's side, sat, and started the engine. Billie, in the passenger seat, pulled down her skirt. She jumped when the cell phone in her purse rang.

She opened her purse for the phone. It read "Raven" on the screen.

"I'm on my way," she said into the phone and then stopped.

"Billie, it's your mother. I've called an ambulance." Raven's voice shook with emotion.

Neil pulled out of the parking lot too quickly for the weather conditions and immediately turned the little sports car toward the beach house where Billie lived.

"What do you mean, you've called the ambulance? What's wrong with her? Turn right here," Billie said as she listened to Raven. "No, that's an alley, it is up a little further."

"I found her on the floor by her bed. She'd fallen out of bed." Raven paused. "She was unresponsive."

Neil pulled into the front yard where the porch light burned, and revolving lights of the emergency vehicle shown like disco lights in the fog. Billie bailed out of the car before he completely stopped, the phone still glued to her ear. The front door opened, and the gurney wheeled out, followed by Raven. A white sheet covered the body completely—no question who lay under the sheet.

****

Lillie let out a howl under the porch as the ambulance drove away. As if by magic, Poppy appeared like a wraith out of the mist and walked to the porch after everyone was gone. He sat down on the ground at the mouth of the hole where the dog lay and patted her head. He spoke softly to the animal that was becoming a mother for the first time in her life and stayed with her until the morning sun began to burn off the shroud that covered the island.

Daylight found four little puppies with their eyes still closed to the world—one black, two brown, and one white.

"You just rest, girl, and I'll get you something to eat." Poppy once again patted the long brown nose as she lay back and let her young nurse. He would take care of her until Billie returned.

Chapter 25

Giselle had planned her own funeral. Practical to a fault, she preferred cremation, and Billie did as her mother asked. Later, they would take the ashes out to sea, but today the funeral held the small group of people from the island who knew Giselle and some old friends from the ballet.

A few old dancers on canes with arthritis in their joints traveled in from out of town. One, a man Billie had never seen before, stayed very attentive to the urn that held her mother. She wondered what secrets her mother took to the grave, but she did not ask.

White lilies adorned the church altar, and a picture of her mother dancing sat next to the urn. The scent of funeral flowers took her back, but she refused to allow those memories to mix with the last thing she would ever do for her mother.

"Miss Billie, I'm so sorry about your mother. She was a good lady." Poppy stood in the church looking out of place in a jacket that had seen better days. Probably it was the only one he owned. After all, who needed a sports coat just to sit on a dock fishing all day? He patted her hand and limped away.

Raven sat up straight in the pew dabbing at her eyes. Billie asked her to sit with the family. On the other side sat Billie's oldest friend, Sandy. She brought her mother and the children.

Once she was home, the neighbors stopped by all afternoon with casseroles and cakes, enough to feed an army. Raven and Sandy stood by taking in the food and finding a place for it. Some would be labeled and frozen for another date.

"So, you have a dog with four pups to keep you company," Martha said with a smile.

"Yes, you want a puppy? In about six weeks I'll be looking for homes. As it is, Poppy is helping me keep them fed."

"Doesn't their mother do that?" Martha looked up from the tea cup she held in her hand.

"Yes, but Mom has to eat so she can feed them. Anyway, Poppy has taken a real shine to Lillie, and maybe he would like to have one of the babies when they are old enough. He might need a companion too."

Billie made the rounds talking to everyone who stopped in, and by afternoon she found she was exhausted.

****

The old house creaked with each gust of wind. Finally, they were gone—everyone gone. Billie had thought she would be pleased when everyone left, and she had time to herself. Now she wasn't sure. She walked from the cleaned and organized kitchen, ushering them all out onto the porch. Sandy would be back later, after she got her mother and kids home.

Taking off the dress she wore to the funeral, she donned shorts and flip flops—the standard uniform of the island. She walked past her mother's room several times and could not make herself go in. From the door, she saw the perfectly made bed. The table showed an empty spot where a lamp once sat, the shattered mess long since swept clean. Billie knew Raven must have cleaned it up after the ambulance left. Only the closet door stood ajar. The room still smelled of her mother's perfume.

Finally, after the third attempt, her footsteps led her into the room. Her mother's dressing table sat as if nothing had ever happened. The mirror she used to see the back of her hair still lay on the lace doily—an antique from another era. It had once belonged to Billie's grandmother. How many women had used it? How many shades of lipstick had been reflected in that mirror? She turned it over running her fingers over the mother-of-pearl back that once held jewels of many colors—now empty slots looked back at Billie, and she wondered what it looked like when new.

When she opened the closet, her mother's scent smacked her in the face once more. The blue robe Mother wore hung on a hook inside the door. What would she do with the clothes now? She should go through them, but her first inclination was to build a fire and burn them. A kind of shrine to all that her mother had been—a dancer, mother, friend, lover. How many labels could you put on a person's life?

"Aunt Billie?"

Billie turned with a start. She had not heard the door open, but Carol stood in the doorway of the bedroom.

"Carol, I didn't hear you come in. Is your mother with you?" Billie closed the closet door quickly and turned to face the girl.

"She's coming. But, I wanted to ask you, if it's okay with my mom, can I have one of Lillie's puppies when they are old enough?" She smiled a young girl smile, looking like her mother in her childhood.

Billie put the mirror back on the dressing table. "Of course, if your mother says it's okay. But it will be about six weeks before they are old enough to eat food and not be dependent up on their mom."

"That's okay, I can wait. What's that? It is so pretty." The girl reached for the mirror on the dresser.

"It belonged to my mother. It had been her mother's. I have no idea what to do with all this stuff, but it is lovely, isn't it?" Billie gestured to the mirror in the girl's hand.

"It looks like Giselle. I can see her using it." Carol smiled as she ran a finger over the handle.

"Would you like to have it to remember Giselle by? I think she would like knowing you have it."

"Really? I can have it?" Carol turned the mirror over and looked at herself in the reflection.

"I want you to. I think Mom would want you to, also." Billie smiled at the girl who was so much like a daughter to her. "Which puppy do you want?" Billie smoothed the doily where the mirror had lay.

"I want a girl dog. I know that much. But I haven't decided which one. Can I go look at them again?" Carol looked up hopefully.

"Yes, but remember to move slowly and speak quietly so not to disturb mother or babies. She has them right under the porch. You can see them from outside."

The girl turned and walked quietly out the door. Billie thought she would be good with a puppy.

Once again inside the closet, Billie saw the hat box. Her mother said it held mementos. She placed the round box on the bed near the window and lifted the lid. Dust motes floated in the afternoon sun as it shone in the window and onto the aging box. There were letters, ribbons, and programs from evenings at the ballet. Her mother's memories, and Billie felt the stab of pain once again. Her mother's entire life in one box on the bed. How would she get through this again?

The pale blue padded envelope lay in the bottom. She gently lifted the lip, and the edges of the paper crumbled in her hands. Inside she found a note written in heavy scrawl, and a black book of matches with gold filigree letters told of bygone days when all the best clubs gave out matchbooks to their patrons. *Johnny Fats*, it read, and she flipped open the cover. The matches were dry and probably still worked. She laid them aside and read the letter.

"My dear Giselle," it read. *"I will never forget the night we met, and I await your answer."*

No signature. Her mother must have known who sent it, or she would not have kept it all these years.

Her mother always said that Billie's father was a dancer who could not marry her. She said no more whenever Billie brought it up. Could he have been the man who sent the note, and if so, what answer did he await? She would never know. Why did she wait so long to open the box, and why the big secret? She and her mother had a beautiful life together, so what did it matter? But she wanted to know.

She fingered the matches as her heart once again ached. It felt like a new cut on top of an old wound that still had not fully healed. And the infection bubbled to the surface.

Chapter 26

Carol carefully knelt and peered under the wooden porch. She could smell the doggy odor of the mother and pups. But they weren't there. Where had they gone? Then she heard the whine deep under the house. Lillie had moved her puppies further back from the sun and possible danger.

Holding her hand up to block the sunlight that shone in her eyes, she looked deep into the dark shade of the porch. Then she stuck her head in, and slowly her eyes began to adjust to the difference in the light. She could see Lillie laying with four puppies attached to her, having a late afternoon snack. Lillie lifted her head to see the intruder and then promptly lay back down breathing out slowly.

Carol lay the precious mirror beside the house. Sliding carefully, she crawled under the porch combat style, using her knees and losing one flip flop along the way. The light filtered through slats and shone on the sand under the porch. Scooting with elbows in sand, slowly she made her way to the dogs.

Lillie lifted her head once more and gave Carol a doggy smile then lay back down. Muffled cries from the babies said they were still hungry when siblings shoved them away. Lillie had plenty for all. Carol lightly stroked the mother's head and then slowly ran a finger down each tiny body as it fed. She thought she might like a girl dog that looked like her mother. If one of the brown ones was a girl, that would be her dog.

****

Billie lifted the ballet program from the hat box and carefully opened the brittle paper. She slid a finger down the list of principal dancers stopping on a faded picture of the woman who now inhabited the urn sitting in the living room. And the knife in her chest twisted.

The room swam, and she grabbed the bedspread like a drowning victim, twisting it in her fingers as she sat. The box and its contents slid off the bed and dumped unceremoniously on the floor. Billie could once again see the bonfire in her mind's eye as she looked at the pile of mementos. She picked up the match book and carefully pulled a match from the cardboard and struck it on the outside—without closing the cover. It bloomed into a red, then yellow flame and quickly burned her finger, but not before catching the others in the book. She stared for a moment before realizing she had dropped the flaming matches into the pile on the floor. The tiny bonfire blazed.

****

The new mother smelled smoke. Her nose lifted up at the floor above her and she knew danger. Lillie stood as best she could under the porch and the pups fell off one at a time complaining. She nosed past the girl who took up most of the room in her new den shoving her out of the way. The girl slid sideways but stayed near the puppies.

Lillie again lifted her nose and smelled the dangerous scent. She had to get her babies somewhere safe. She crawled back under the porch and grabbed the closest puppy's neck in her mouth and crawled back out into the light. She looked around and until she saw the car that always sat by the house. She could hear the girl call her name, as she once again slid under the house for the next baby.

"Lillie, where are you going? Where are you taking your babies?" The girl lifted her head as if she also smelled the danger and tried to turn around.

With baby number two under the car, Lillie went back under again. This time the girl had turned and lay in her way, but she had the two remaining puppies in her hand holding them out to the dog. She yelled and banged on the floor above her when Lillie took one more pup out into the open.

****

When Jake and Sandy arrived at the house they heard yelling from the side of the house. Smoke oozed out the open front door and from the end of the porch. Sandy ran for the house calling her best friend's name. Billie was most likely in the house—and maybe her daughter.

The smoke came from Giselle's bedroom, and after the thorough cleaning of Billie's kitchen, Sandy knew where the fire extinguisher sat. The house was small; she ran through the bungalow to the kitchen in the back and then up front to the open bedroom, thanking the Air Force for the mandatory annual fire extinguisher training she had taken for years.

As she ran through the door to Giselle's bedroom she saw nothing but a bed smoldering until she rounded the end. There sat her best friend in the world staring at the flaming pile of trash on the wooden floor as the bed smoldered and then caught. Bright flames licked up the side of the bed as a light breeze blew past the open window oblivious of the activity inside. It sucked the flames to the window catching the curtains.

Sandy pulled the pin and aimed at the base of the flames squeezing the trigger of the extinguisher covering everything with the white foam.

****

Carol twisted to give the puppy to his mother when the pain pierced her shoulder. Something above her held her captive. She once again twisted and cried out in pain. Lillie took the puppy from her and again left her alone under the house—unable to move with the lone pup in her hand. Suddenly someone yelled her name from the opening under the house. Jake! He found her!

"Carol!" Her big brother called out as he stuck his head under the porch. "Are you under here? The house is on fire you have to get out!"

He yanked on her bare foot and she screamed kicking out at him. "I'm stuck on something." She felt the warm blood running down her arm as she tried to back out. "My shirt is hooked on a nail or something. I think I'm bleeding." She tried not to whine. She knew her brother hated it when she whined.

Jake slithered under the porch as it became more and more smoky in the enclosed area. He coughed once or twice. Carol knew Jake had allergies even though he tried not to admit to it.

Lillie appeared beside him slithering along on her belly to Carol's side. Carol still held her last baby in her hand. The underneath side of the porch became very crowded as the smoke thickened.

"I found it. Your blouse is stuck on a nail. I'm going to tear it lose. We have to get out of here before we burn up too." Jake gave orders to his sister as usual.

"Where's Mom and Aunt Billie?" The pup in Carol's hand whimpered when its mother came near.

"Mom ran in the house. I don't know where Aunt Billie is, but we have to get out of here." Jake ripped the cloth from the nail scratching his hand in the process. "Come on!"

Jake twisted and crawled toward the entrance, Carol right behind him, when Lillie got in between them nosing Carol's hand. She gave the dog her final pup and then slithered out behind her.

Once out into the sunlight, Carol grabbed the mirror and then turned to see the smoke that now billowed out of the door she left open. She ran for the house and her mother.

****

Billie became aware of someone else in the room. A blast of cold froze the flames on the floor and bedspread. She found herself jerked to a standing position; someone yelled into her blank face. Sandy. Where had she come from and why the yelling? Billie felt herself grabbed roughly by the arm and dragged from her mother's room, through the house, and out the door. Tears streamed down her face, and her eyes stung from smoke.

Shoved off the porch, she saw Carol and Jake coming around the corner covered in dirt except for a bloody spot on Carol's shoulder. What had happened and why couldn't she remember?

Chapter 27

When she awoke, the sun shone through clear glass making her squint. The room smelled of disinfectant, and the bed was not hers. She wore yellow institutional pajamas under a green cotton blanket and a needle protruded from her hand. When she looked up, she saw the IV pole hung above her head—then the door opened with a bang.

"Oh, you're awake." The nurse—barely out of her teens—wore pink printed scrubs and clogs on her feet. The stethoscope hung around her neck and her name tag said L. Terry, RN. She must have been older than she looked.

L. Terry, RN, went about the business of checking vitals as Billie wiped the sleep from her eyes. She remembered Sandy taking her to the hospital. She was insistent, but gentle. She remembered begging her friend not to leave her, then things became foggy. Something in the back of her mind reminded her of a fire, but she couldn't quite put her finger on it. A bonfire at her home. No, a bonfire in her home. Did the house burn down? She showed no signs of burns.

"Ms. Stone, how are you feeling this morning? Do you remember being admitted last night?" Nurse Terry flipped the stethoscope back around her neck.

"Yes, I remember being admitted, but I'm fuzzy as to why."

"Well, you're here for observation under Dr. Flint's care. Do you know Dr. Flint?" The nurse eyed her carefully.

"Yes, she is my psychiatrist. Has she been in to see me?" Billie tried to sit up in the bed; the hand with the needle gave her trouble.

"Yes, she's been in, and she has you scheduled for a session today. I understand you attempted suicide in your home yesterday." The nurse reached up and squeezed the almost empty IV bag.

"No. I'm sure I didn't. You must be mistaken."

"Do you remember starting a fire in your home?" The nurse helped her sit up and then adjusted the bed and pillow behind her.

"A fire? No. Oh yes, I was going through my mother's things. We had her funeral, and I was trying to clean up afterwards. But I don't think I tried to kill myself. Was there a fire?"

The nurse nodded.

"And the girl? Carol, is she okay?" Bits and pieces were beginning to fall into place for Billie. She did remember the hat box of mementos and the book of matches. But she didn't strike them, did she?

The door opened, and Dr. Flint walked in with a file in her hand.

"How are you feeling, Billie?" The light scent of lavender wafted from the woman with kind yet knowing eyes.

"A little fuzzy, but okay."

"I want to see you later today after lunch. We'll talk about what happened at home yesterday. You've been under a huge stress with the funeral and everything, and we need to discuss what transpired and how you feel about it. Okay?"

Billie nodded.

The doctor wrote in the file and handed it to the nurse. "Okay, Billie, we'll meet after lunch." She smiled and left the room.

Billie wished she could remember what she had done to end up in the hospital. The nurse gently removed the needle from her hand and put a tiny band-aid over the wound.

"I'll be back with your lunch tray," she said and left the room.

****

"So, you say you had no intention of ending your life?" Dr. Flint sat in the room reserved for consultations. She crossed her legs and took off her glasses, staring at Billie, making her self-conscious.

Billie fidgeted in her seat. "Dr. Flint, I know the nurse thought I tried to commit suicide. Maybe my friend Sandy did too. I remember so little of it, but I don't think that was my intention. I wanted to get rid of the things in my mother's house, or maybe I wanted a bonfire in her memory. I know that sounds stupid, but those are the thoughts I remember having, not ending my life as you say."

"Well, how do you feel about what you've done?" The doctor looked up from the pad where she took notes.

"Like I said, it was stupid. Maybe I had an incident of bad judgment, but I didn't want to die. I don't want to die. I want to get better."

The doctor again wrote on the pad. "I'm going to increase your anti-anxiety meds for now. If all goes well, we'll reduce the dosage later, but for now, let's be careful. You've had a great shock to add to the other problems you already had. You recently had an episode with Joe Franks and then your mother's funeral after a break-in. I want to be careful. Your friend Sandy tells me she will be around for a while. Also, you have her mother, and the people you work with. I want you not to be alone for a while. I need you to stay today for observation, and if things are good, I'll release you tomorrow. Once home, stay busy and see me again in a week. Does that seem like a good idea to you?"

"Yes. I want to go home, and I'll be sure to surround myself with help."

"Good. I'll see to your release tomorrow, and I'll see you again before you leave. Then I want you back in my office next week for a meeting. Take the meds and call me if there are any problems."

Billie shook her head.

Chapter 28

Once again on the island after leaving Billie in the capable hands of the hospital staff, Sandy walked into the house that smelled of smoke. How had she not seen this coming—how could she have not seen the effects of the funeral on Billie? She should have realized when her mother's death came so quickly, but Billie appeared to be handling it so well.

Sandy left Billie in the care of a hospital on the mainland, and they called her therapist. Billie had been admitted and would be kept for a few days. Sandy would go back and get her when they released her. They were calling Billie's breakdown an incident, not an attempted suicide. Sandy was not sure, but she hoped they were right. She only knew she had almost lost her best friend and her daughter in one giant mess. She could not bear to think about those results.

On the floor, next to Giselle's charred bed lay the pile of burned mementos. Blackened rubbish piled on the equally blackened wooden floor. Walking to the back porch, Sandy found the broom and dustpan. She would sweep up the memories of a woman who lived a long life, a woman she loved, and simply throw them away. A tear ran down her cheek as she brushed the charred remains into a pile. The hat box lay beside it unscathed. Leaning over she found the program from long ago—brittle and yellow—and now with a corner burned away—leaving the picture of the prima ballerina on pointe looking longingly toward the camera. Billie's mother danced to her namesake as the lead dancer in the ballet *Giselle*. How could Sandy simply throw this into the trash like Giselle never lived? If Billie came home and found her mother's things again, would it trigger another episode?

She piled the least charred papers into the hat box and took them to the back porch, then swept up the remainder. Returning to the bedroom, she took down the ragged curtains and piled them on the bed, rolling up the bedding and carrying it out the back door where the trash cans sat. Uncle Paul would come by soon and help her dispose of the mattress and box springs. The antique bed frame might still be salvageable for someone who wanted to refinish it.

Next on the list she wanted to make sure Lillie's pups were safe and their mother well-fed. Walking toward the front of the small house she heard a tentative knock. Poppy stood by the front door, hat in hand.

"Hello, Poppy. Please come in." She opened the door and ushered him in. He looked uncomfortable when not sitting in his place on the dock.

"Hello Miss Sandy. Is Miss Billie back home yet?" He looked around the room eyes glancing at everything.

"No, not yet. But soon I hope. What can I do for you?" Nothing escaped Poppy on Sandhill Island, but then most of the island knew what happened. Gossip spread faster than the fire in the bedroom that day—and some of it even accurate.

"Nuthin', really. I was just checking on things. I had been helping Miss Billie with the dog and her pups and just wondered if I could still do that? Miss Billie and her mother were really good people, and I want to help them if I can."

"Yes, they were. Billie still is." She nodded toward Billie's bedroom door like the woman stood there. "As a matter of fact, I need to feed Lillie. I think she is still under the car with her babies. I hoped to be able to get her to move to the front porch, but I don't know if she will."

"Maybe if you made a bed for her? Dogs are funny. They'll move when they're ready, not when you are ready."

"I know. I doubt she'll ever go back under the house with the pups after the fire. Can you help me make her a place on the front porch? Maybe she would feel comfortable under the swing or somewhere out of the way of prying eyes. I hate knowing she is just under the car."

"Of course, Miss Sandy. You know I'd do anything for you and Miss Billie." Poppy smiled an almost toothless smile—one that had probably never seen a dentist.

"Good, come with me." Sandy led Poppy to the back porch that doubled as the utility room. In the corner was an almost new hot water heater. On the back wall, the washer and dryer were surrounded by cabinets. Sandy knew rags were stored in those cabinets. The first door she opened held ragged bedding and towels. Giselle came from an older generation who saved things—unlike the throw-away generation of today. Loading her arms with soft bedding for the dog, Sandy handed them to Poppy and led him back to the front porch.

"Do you think she would be comfortable under the

swing? We'll have to warn everyone to not sit there for the next few weeks. Here, help me raise the chain so it's a little higher off the ground." Sandy unhooked the chain and raised it a few notches as Poppy did the same on the other side. Now with the swing too high to use, it might give Lillie a sense of security.

Sandy knelt and spread the ragged blanket on the floor, then reached up for the towels that Poppy still held in his hands. Unfolding them, she laid them on top, knowing the dog would rearrange them to her satisfaction.

With a container of dry dog food in hand, Sandy walked to the car which sat next to the house unused on most days. Kneeling down, she looked under. Lillie smiled at her. She lay on her side with the four pups shoving for a place—each one certain the other sibling had the best vantage point. Sweet grunts came from under the car as the mother lay calmly allowing her babies to feed. Slowly the pups fell off after filling their tiny bellies and curled up next to mom in a puppy pile ready for an afternoon nap.

"Hey Lillie." Sandy spoke softly to the new mother who probably felt abandoned after Billie left. Sandy gently held out a morsel of food to the exhausted mother. "How about a snack, honey?" Lillie carefully took the nibble of food from Sandy's hand. Sandy allowed her to chew it and then offered another, not reaching as far under the car this time so the dog would have to stretch for it. She patted the velvet head each time the dog took a piece and gave her plenty of time to eat each piece. Slowly Sandy backed up forcing the dog to slide out after the snack. Then Sandy left a trail of dog food leading to the front porch where the new doggie nest lay snuggled in the corner under the safety of the swing. Sandy looked around and spied the meditation rocks. They would prop the front door open and leave it that way, so Lillie could come and go. Surely, after the fire, Lillie would think the porch a safer home for her new babies.

Sandy sat on the chair next to the front door of the house and waited—Poppy still outside near the door. Slowly the velvet brindle muzzle showed around the corner of the screen door and looked quizzically at Sandy. Then one paw stepped gingerly up on the porch.

"That's right, Lillie girl. Come on in and check out the new bed. It will be so nice to get your babies out of the dirt. And I'll leave the door open, so you can come and go. You'll even have your dog bowls next to the bed. It will be more comfortable for you and your new family." Sandy's steady sing-song voice soothed the skittish dog, and she followed the dog food trail toward the bed.

"Poppy, can you reach the babies and bring them to the new bed?" Sandy nodded to the man who helped her.

"Sure, Miss Sandy." His head disappeared as he squatted beside the car. Sandy could not see him, but he grunted as he struggled underneath. Soon he crawled out with tiny puppies wiggling in his arms.

"Just put them on the bed," she instructed as he stepped up on the porch. "If Mom doesn't want them there, she'll take them back where she had them."

Lillie made small woofing sounds as she stood up on hind legs to see her babies cradled in Poppy's arms. Poppy bent down on old crackling knees and gently placed the puppies on the new bedding, Lillie right behind him. The dog crawled under the swing sniffing each pup, then lay down with them, bathing each one.

"Well, let's see if she keeps them there. Poppy, thank you for your help." Sandy patted his arm.

"Happy to help," he replied as he took the dog's water bowl and dumped it outside in the sand then walked to the faucet, refilled it with cool, fresh water, and placed it back on the porch. "Dogs like fresh water," he said simply and then walked away.

Sandy knew he would be back. She walked back through the front door to the house to see what else she could do for Billie and to give Lillie and her new family some time alone.

Chapter 29

The familiar scent of lavender threatened to make her vomit. At first, she found it soothing, but now, it made her want to heave.

"Could we turn off the diffuser?" Billie pointed to the machine that sat on the table with steam coming from its top.

"Of course. I didn't know it bothered you. Most of my clients like it." Dr. Flint switched off the knob on the side of the diffuser. "It will take a while to dissipate."

"I used to like it but for some reason, it is making me sick today." Billie sat on the edge of the couch unable to relax.

"Are you sick of coming here?" The doctor sat down and crossed her legs, then picked up the pad and pen that lay beside her chair.

"No. Well, maybe yes. I don't mean any disrespect. You've done me so much good. I could never have survived without your help. As my mother would say, I'm sick and tired of being sick and tired. I want to get well, and I want to stay that way." Without thinking, Billie slid back in the seat and folded her hands.

"That's a big step. Do you think you are well?" Dr. Flint made notes on the tablet.

"I don't know if I'll ever be well—or at least the same as I used to be. But I know I am tired of being a victim and tired of people tip-toeing around me like they are afraid I'll break. I just want to be normal again." Billie stared off into space

"And what is normal?" the doctor asked.

"I'm not sure. I thought I was normal once, before the accident. I know life will never be the same without my family, but I just want to be happy again and to move on." Billie folded her legs into a yoga position placing her hands on her knees. This position, once alien, had become comfortable lately.

"The fact that you want to be happy again is a big step. Your family is gone and now your mother, too. You have learned a lot about dealing with loss." The doctor took off her glasses and looked at Billie.

"I have learned to accept it, I guess. Like you said I've learned to accept my imperfections and the loss of my family. My entire family now. All I have left is my dog. But she is a great companion. Well, I also have friends too."

"Yes, your friend, Sandy, who brought you in to the emergency room, she is a great resource. But I understand she lives in Biloxi and is not around all the time." The doctor smoothed her pants, then looked up at Billie.

"No, she's not. But I have other friends on the island. Sandy's mom, Martha, her Uncle Paul, Sam, the chef at Le Chez where I work, String, the other musician I work with, and now Neil, the man I told you about. They are always around and very protective."

"When I met you in the emergency room you were attempting suicide, but yet you think you are better now." The room became deathly quiet and the women looked at each other across the room.

"I didn't think of it that way. I don't think I meant to die. I don't remember a lot of what happened, but I had an image in my mind of a bonfire. I thought of building a bonfire in my mother's memory—or maybe removing the memories that hurt me when I looked at them. Yes, a bonfire in the house was not a good idea. But I really don't think I wanted to die."

"Do you think you made good decisions there? I mean with a bonfire?" The doctor leaned a little closer to Billie.

"No, obviously not. But I had just discovered something about my mother. I don't know for sure what… I think, I may have a father who is alive. I found a note that said the person who wrote it awaited her answer. It looked like a man's handwriting. I wondered if it might have been my father. As a child, I asked about my father, but my mother always said the same thing. She said he was a dancer who could not marry her. Now I wonder. If he awaited her answer, maybe he asked her to marry him, and she turned him down. I wish I'd asked more questions, but I didn't. She made it clear with her tone of voice, the conversation had ended."

"Are you going to try to find out who your father is? And what will you do with this information if you do find out? After all your mother died an old woman; you need to realize, Billie, even if you find your father, he might not be alive."

"Yes, I realize that. My mother was fair skinned with blue eyes and light hair when young. I obviously have dark hair, skin and eyes. I could have gotten that from my father. A man attended the funeral who hung around the urn with her ashes a very long time. I wondered who he was. He came with a group of retired dancers from the mainland. I know it is silly, but what if he could be my father? I mean I just had a feeling about him."

"Well, again, what would you do with the information now if you had it? But if you are really interested, contact those people who were at the funeral and ask them. They had known your mother a long time. However, you need to realize he could not be in your life all those years, and even if you do find him, he still might not want to be a part of your life. But back to the subject of you, now that you are back home, and your mother and Raven are gone, you said all you have left is your dog and some friends. How do you plan to spend your days when you're not working?"

"First, I am going to clean out the house of my mother's things. Sandy has promised to help me this time. I think I will make my mother's bedroom a music room. I want a piano again, now that there is room for one. I want to write my own music, not just sing someone else's." Billie looked at the doctor who had treated her all these years.

"You write music too?" The doctor appeared surprised.

"I always have—well I used to, but not since the accident. I would like to get back into it."

"That's a wonderful idea. I believe the creation of things is always healing. I think humans were made to create. And to hide that creativity is to hide a good portion of the person. I'm happy to hear you say that. I think it could be a major step forward."

Chapter 30

Both women stood by the car and watched the water as the ferry made its way from the mainland. Billie had only been gone a few days, but it seemed like years. She breathed deeply the salty air.

"You took care of Lillie?" Billie turned to look at her long-time friend knowing the answer before it came.

"Of course. I even moved her. Well, Poppy and I did. He's been very attentive to Lillie and the puppies, and he keeps wanting to know what he can do for you."

"Moved her where?" The wind blew Billie's long dark hair into her face, and she pushed it aside with her fingers.

"She and the babies are set up on the porch under the swing on a pallet. I used some rags from the utility room as bedding. I've washed them every other day to get rid of the puppy smell, but she has stayed. Oh, and Poppy and I raised the swing a little to give her more room; that way no one will try to sit in it. After the puppies are gone, we can move her bed out from under the swing and put it back to its original height."

"You've been working! I can't believe you got her inside." The wind once again whipped Billie's hair— this time the other direction.

"Well, she moved the pups under the car, and I wanted to find a better place for her. I doubted she

162

would go back under the house after the smoke ran her out."

"I can't believe I did that. I can't believe I almost burned the house down with Carol and Lillie underneath—and me inside." Billie breathed heavily.

"Well, there's no going back. It happened. Now we move forward—and no one was hurt." Sandy held her hand up to shade her eyes and looked toward the island.

"Sandy, I'm so sorry. It scares me so much to think what could have happened. And poor Carol. You know I love your kids like they are my own. I'd never hurt them." A tear ran down her face and she brushed it away wiping it into her blowing hair.

Sandy put her arm around her friend. "I know that, and so does Carol. What is important now is to get you well. You and the doctor talked, and you told her it wasn't a suicide attempt, right?"

"Yes, I told her I didn't want to die. I kept thinking of a bonfire in my mother's honor. And there were matches and…"

"Well, no more bonfires inside or out. Okay?" Sandy raised one eyebrow then held up her little finger for her friend. They linked fingers, and both said, "pinky swear," at the same time.

"Sandy, when I went through my mother's things that day, I found a note in the box where she kept mementos. It looked like a man's handwriting. It said something about awaiting her decision. She had kept it all these years, and I wondered if the note came from my father. My mom always said he was a dancer who could not marry her. I wondered if the decision concerned me. What if he asked her to marry him? Am I being crazy? Again? I mean, what if he is still alive?

Did you see the older people from the ballet who came to the service? One of the men hung around Mom's urn forever. I would like to find him."

"Well, I plan to stay here this summer until I have to go back for the job. I cleaned up the mess in your mother's room and put the unburned paper into the hat box out in the utility room. I didn't throw away anything except the charred bed clothes. We can look through them again—together this time in case you have another fire starter episode—and then we can ask around. Poppy seems to know everyone. We could start there." The ferry began heading for port and the women climbed back into Sandy's car. "And I'll help you get the rest of your mother's things out of the house or put away. Oh, by the way, Aunt Patti, Paul's wife, would like to buy the bedroom suite if you want to sell. She loves to refinish furniture."

"Actually, I do. I told Dr. Flint I would like to buy a piano and move it into my mother's old room. I want to renovate her bedroom and make it into a music room. I want to start composing again."

Sandy glanced at her friend as she pulled off the ferry and turned toward the house. "Billie, that's wonderful! Uncle Paul said he would sand and refinish the floor. He thinks it can be salvaged."

Billie smiled and looked toward the ocean. "And paint the walls a calm, Caribbean blue. I love it. I'm ready to get back to the business of living again."

Chapter 31

The next few days were spent organizing and cleaning out Giselle's things. Sandy spent most of her days with Billie—unwilling to let her do the job alone. One bonfire was enough, and even though Billie felt okay, Sandy worried. She knew she'd have to go home someday, but not yet.

Paul left the shrimping to the crew and took part of one day sanding the wooden floor and then began the refinishing job. Poppy checked on Lillie and her pups, whose eyes were beginning to open, at least twice a day. Life calmed down to a dull roar.

"Mom!" Jake called as he ran in the front door of Billie's house. They took the kids swimming in the afternoons, and even Jake glowed with a golden tan. For some reason, the kids didn't fight like they used to. Sandy thought staying with Grandma on the island away from the everyday stress could be good for a family.

"In the bedroom, Jake." Sandy called back.

His long frame swung around the corner of the door facing and he stopped.

"Wow." He surveyed the room with childlike eyes that were quickly turning into a young man's. He didn't have his nose in an electronic game and saw the reality before him. "You've done a lot of work."

The room was empty of furniture, even the closet

had been cleaned out of all clothing. A few things were stored in the cabinets on the back porch along with the hat box of mementos while Billie prepared her music room. The walls held a fresh coat of paint—a calm Caribbean blue. The closet door stood open, and Billie leafed through sheet music and placed it on the shelves.

"Hey Jakie." Billie always called him that baby name, and he said he hated it. She wondered now if he enjoyed the extra attention she gave him with his nickname. "Your sister with you?"

"She's on the porch with Lillie and the puppies. I think she's finally picked out the one she wants. I don't know if she's named her yet or not. Are we going swimming? Grandma made us eat lunch, and we have our suits on and towels packed." Jake knew the routine.

"Sunscreen?" his mother responded as she stood back and looked at the curtains she just hung.

"Check!" Jake smiled at his Mom.

"Jake you're getting a tan. I told you that you could tan through a 100 SPF." Sandy smiled at her son who looked so much like his father, the man who was no longer her husband. It sometimes made it difficult to deal with the son who resembled her ex so much. But he wasn't entirely his father's child.

"Every now and then you're right." Jake looked at his mom with ice blue eyes and then turned to go. "Are you about finished so we can go to the beach?"

"I think so." Sandy adjusted the gathers in the curtains one last time.

"Well, get dressed!" Jake shouted in anticipation.

Sandy lifted her top to show she already had her swimsuit on underneath. She knew the drill.

Out on the porch Carol cradled her new puppy. It

wiggled as she stroked its tiny body, and Lillie reached up giving it a motherly lick. "She's so cute! I can't wait to take her home." Carol held the pup up to her face and they bumped noses.

"Well, let her have some lunch while we go to the beach." Sandy and Jake walked out the front door of the house and onto the porch. Lillie looked relaxed and happy with her little family of four on the pallet under the swing. Carol once again kissed the top of her new puppy's head and placed her lovingly back with her mom.

The door slammed behind Billie as she emerged from the house with an ice chest, heading for the beach.

"I'm going to try to catch Poppy this afternoon and see if he knows who the dancers were that came to Mom's funeral. If he knows the name of the man who seemed so upset over Mom's death, maybe I can find him." Billie looked at her friend as she munched on the sandwiches packed for them. "Do you think that's a good idea?" Billie pulled down the straps to her suit and let them hang on her arms. "I'm getting tan lines and they look funny with the dresses I work in."

"Tan lines don't show with a flight suit. Anyway, I see nothing wrong with it if you think it's a good idea. Talk to Poppy. He knows everything. I mean, I knew my father, and I really don't know what it would be like to grow up without one, but it seems strange to me that you never had any interest in knowing him until now." Sandy took a drink from her water bottle. Squeals could be heard from the water as the kids splashed in the surf.

"I guess it's just that since Mom is gone I feel more alone. I have lots of friends and a support group, but no family. I don't know why I think that's important, but I do. I just wish I had asked more questions while she lived." Billie pulled the lettuce that hung from her sandwich and stuffed it in her mouth.

"Well, if you think it's important, then I do too. And I'm sure you're right about not talking to a person enough when they are alive. I'm sure when the time comes I'll want to talk to Mom and she won't be around." Sandy looked out counting heads in the water and waved the kids back closer to shore.

"Oh, are you busy on Thursday? I want to go to Corpus Christi and look at pianos. Come with me? We can pack up the kids and your mom if she wants to go and have some lunch while we're there." Billie wiped her mouth with the paper towels packed for the picnic.

"Sounds great. I'll check with Mom. Billie, I am so happy to see you getting back into your music. You have such a talent, and I think you should use it. And it might be what makes the healing process go more smoothly." She shoved the scraps of her lunch into the plastic bag and tossed it into the ice chest with the rest of the trash, then stood and walked toward the water.

"Mom! Look what I found!" Carol called from knee deep in the water and pointing into the clear blue ocean.

****

Poppy dumped the water bowl that sat on the porch next to Lillie's pallet into the sandy soil out front. Refilling it, he stepped back up on the porch as Billie emerged from the house.

"Hey, Poppy. How are you today? I didn't hear you when you came in this morning." Billie stood barefoot in shorts with her hair pulled back in a ponytail. "Would you like a glass of tea?"

"Well, that'd be real nice, Miss Billie. I'll take it out on the porch with Lillie if that's okay." He shifted uncomfortably. "I like to be outside during the day."

"It's a beautiful day. Lemon and sugar?" Billie brushed a stray hair out of her face.

"Yes, thank ye. I'll be here with the dogs." He leaned down on arthritic knees and patted Lillie on the head as she watched her pups sleep.

Billie handed the glass of tea to Poppy and sat in the chair next to the door gesturing to the one next to her. Poppy sat.

"Would you like to have a puppy when they are old enough to leave their mother?" Billie eyed the man who took such good care of her dog.

"Well, Miss Billie, I've been wanting to ask that very question, if you don't already have homes for all of them. I'd take good care of it and all." He took a gulp of tea.

"I know you would, Poppy. Carol has picked out the brown female pup, but other than that one, none are spoken for. You can have the pick of the litter except for Carol's dog." A broad smile formed on Poppy's face, and he looked at the pups with their mother as they woke hungry and began to nurse before the afternoon nap. Billie was sure he was weighing his options and deciding which pup to take.

"Poppy, I've wanted to ask you a question for a while now. You know everyone on the island, and you knew my mother." Billie took a sip of tea.

"Yes. Miss Giselle, she was a real nice lady." Poppy pulled his eyes away from the dogs, drank the tea deeply, and then wiped his mouth with his sleeve.

"Yes. I wondered… At the funeral, I saw a man in

a white hat and suit; he leaned on a cane, and he spent a lot of time at the funeral next to Mom's urn. I think he came from Corpus Christi with the dancers Mom knew when young. Do you know who he was?"

"You mean Rico? Your mother's boyfriend?" Another gulp of tea and he almost drained the glass.

Billie's glass slipped from her wet fingers and she grabbed it with the other hand, spilling some of it on her lap and the floor. She brushed at the wet spot on her shorts with the towel that lay on the table between them and then wiped up the liquid on the floor. "My mother had a boyfriend?"

"Um, was I not supposed to say that? I didn't know it was a secret. He came to the island sometimes, but you would have been in school. So, you probably didn't see him." One final drink and he emptied his glass.

"How about another glass?" Billie stood with her half empty glass and reached for Poppy's.

"If it's not too much trouble." Poppy smiled again as he handed her the empty glass. "You make some real good tea, Miss Billie—just like your mother used to."

"Thank you, I'll be right back." Billie walked into her kitchen and stood at the sink as she tried to dry her shorts on a clean tea towel. Her mother had a boyfriend. And he came to the island while she went to school. Billie remembered her mother going to Corpus Christi three days a week to teach at the Corpus Christi Concert Ballet Academy as Artistic Director. On those days, Billie walked home to Sandy's house after school and stayed until her mother got home. If she had visitors on the days she didn't work, Billie never knew it. Would Martha have known? And if so did the rest of the island? Billie knew there had always been secrets on

Sandhill Island, but she wasn't aware that her mother held one of them.

She suddenly realized that she had done nothing about refilling the tea glasses and promptly pulled the pitcher from the refrigerator. Adding sugar and lemon to Poppy's glass, she stepped back out onto the porch.

Poppy sat on the floor of the porch with the black puppy in his lap.

"I think I'll name him Blackie." He gently petted the black-as-midnight dog. Billie thought the dog a perfect choice for one who would spend most days outside with Poppy on the dock while his master fished.

"A perfect name." She asked no more questions. She had a name for the man at her mother's funeral, and she would begin at the Corpus Christi Concert Ballet. Maybe someone there still knew Rico and her mother. Maybe when they looked at pianos on Thursday, they could make a little detour. But first, she would talk to Martha.

Chapter 32

"So, you knew Mom had a boyfriend?" Billie looked Martha up and down. "And you never told me?"

Martha placed her knitting into the basket at her feet and patted Billie's arm. "Honey, you were too young. And later, if your mother had wanted you to know, she would have told you. He danced with the ballet on the mainland—I bumped into him a few times. You know how small this island is, and everyone knows everyone. But I didn't talk about it. Your mother had her own life. She came to the island with you when you were just a baby. We all knew she taught dancing—she made her living that way. I thought her wonderful, and that was all I needed to know about her."

"But my father, why didn't he marry her? Did she not want to get married or were there other reasons?" Billie sat on Martha's front porch. Her conversation with Poppy the other day had stirred a lot of emotions. Sandy had taken the kids to the grocery store with promises of letting them pick out some of the week's meals, probably to give Billie and Martha time to talk.

"Did you know his last name?" Billie brushed at imaginary crumbs on her T-shirt.

"Santori or something? No, Santiago. Rico Santiago. I remember thinking how exotic—at least for Texas. It surprised me that he came to the funeral. He's an old man now, like the rest of us. I thought it wonderful that the dancers from Corpus came to pay their respects." Martha looked up as Sandy's van pulled in to the yard. The doors flew open, and kids spilled out running for the porch.

"Groceries! You have to help bring in the groceries." Sandy called to the kids who turned around and walked back to the car listlessly. One minute they were running free, and the next they were indentured servants.

"Look, Aunt Billie, I got new flip flops!" Carol showed off pink flip flops from the grocery store. She had been in tennis shoes since the fire when she came out from under the house with only one. No one wanted to go back under to look for the lost one.

"Very nice. Let's get these groceries put away, and then we can go piano shopping. What do you say?"

****

The kids stood at the railing of the ferry as they crossed to the mainland. Martha sat in the van with Billie in the back seat.

"I didn't mean to upset you, Martha. I was just surprised about my mother's boyfriend, and I want to try to talk to him, if I can." Sandy looked out at the gulls on their never-ending search for food.

"You didn't upset me, dear. I guess I just never thought about talking to you about it—so long ago." Martha turned around to see the woman who had been like a second daughter to her.

"I found a note in a box of mementos—before the bonfire incident—and I wondered what question he asked, but Mom always said my father was a dancer who could not marry her. I never asked too many questions. Now that she's gone, I would like to know who my father is—or who he used to be. I've lost my entire family and would really like to talk to Rico. Maybe he is and maybe he isn't my father, but he cared about Mom, I know. I could tell by the way he acted at the funeral. I'd like to stop by the ballet today while we are in Corpus, if we have time, and see if anyone knows how to find him."

Sandy called her kids back to the van where they waited their turn to leave the ferry and drive onto the mainland of Corpus Christi. Billie had a list of piano stores and promised them they would eat at a restaurant when they got hungry. Sandy had packed snacks knowing the kids were always hungry, hoping to stave off the whining for food while they shopped.

****

The artificially cool store played piped-in music in the huge hall. The gleaming floors held pianos of all types and styles from grands to baby grands and uprights. They even had electric pianos for those inclined to that style. Billie knew what she wanted, and she did not have room for a grand.

She ran her fingers over the finish of the concert grand piano pushed ceremoniously to the front of the store. The good stuff sat up front. Never in her wildest dreams could she afford such an instrument.

A woman in stiletto heels and tight skirt emerged from the back as Sandy shushed her kids. They were allowed electronics today to keep them occupied.

"It has an exceptional sound. Do you play?" She eyed Billie, who stood by the piano in a long flowing skirt and sandals. Her hair pulled back in a clip to deal with the humidity, she wore no jewelry and little makeup. Billie didn't look like the high roller type who would buy the piano she touched gingerly.

"Yes, I play. I'm looking for a piano for the house. I wouldn't have room for this." She ran her fingers over the ivory keys, and the sound reverberated through the room.

"We have the baby grands and one petite grand in the back." The woman looked at Martha and the children, then back to Billie. "We also have some used items that have been traded in."

"What are the prices on the smaller ones?" Billie looked around the room and walked toward a smaller version of the magnificent instrument up front.

"I'll get you a price list. Of course, the prices can be negotiated, and we have a finance plan." She looked Billie up and down then turned to retrieve the price list.

"I doubt I can afford these," Billie whispered to Sandy once the woman left the room.

"Well, they're not the only store in town." Sandy moved quickly toward Jake who walked fast in the direction of the electric piano near the wall. "No," was all she said.

In the corner sat a petite version of the piano, about four or five feet wide, at the front. She lifted the lid that covered the keys and ran her fingers over them, then placed her finger on middle C and began her rendition of *Summertime* from *Porgy and Bess*. She caressed keys that felt smooth as buttered silk, humming under her breath as she played.

"Jazz, huh? Very nice." The sales woman reappeared near Billie's elbow with a price list in her hand.

"Yes, I'm a jazz singer and want to get back into

composition." Billie pulled the lid back down over the keys.

"I can make you a good deal on that. It has been gently used. She handed the price sheet to Billie after circling the instrument on the paper, then wrote a figure off the side. She reached into her pocket and pulled out a business card.

"Thank you. I just started looking. I'll get back to you." Billie took the papers and placed them in her bag.

"Well, come back and see me after you've shopped. We'll talk. We have the best instruments on the Gulf." The woman smiled as Billie took the paperwork.

Billie could hear the kids starting to get noisy. It was time to go. "Thank you, I will."

Back in the van, they drove to the few music stores Billie had on her list. She found several great pianos, and none of them were cheap. Her goal to own a piano again would be hard on the budget.

Billie played several pianos in the stores they visited and as usual, the sales people saw talent. Talent they wanted to tap—and sell to.

"Jake, stop it!" Carol turned and shoved her brother who walked behind her stepping on the new flip flops.

"Okay, enough. Jake leave your sister alone. Let's wait outside." Sandy turned her children and pushed them toward the door. Martha followed.

Billie could see that the kids were tired of shopping. Maybe she should have made this trip alone, but she had promised them lunch. She quickly thanked the sales person and turned toward the door.

"Okay, who likes Snoopy's Pier?" Billie knew the restaurant wasn't far, and the kids could have a break before one more stop.

"I do!" Carol shouted.

"Cool." Jake almost looked up from the game on his phone.

"What do you say, Mom and Grandma? Want some lunch?" Billie looked at her friends. Martha mopped her brow with an embroidered hanky that Billie knew she had stitched many years ago. How many people actually carried handkerchiefs these days? Or embroidered them. Billie felt so close to Martha. She needed to be sure she hadn't hurt the older woman's feelings with accusing her of not mentioning Rico before.

"Sounds good to me," Martha said, and Sandy nodded.

"I've got the GPS coordinates, Mom." Jake handed his phone over the back seat. "In case you need directions."

"Are you hungry, Jake?" Sandy took the phone and sat it in the center console of the car.

"Always," he answered honestly.

Chapter 33

Snoopy's specialized in fresh seafood and an ice cream/dessert bar. They found a place in the shade near the water with a fan blowing on the table. Martha did not take the heat well. Unused to air conditioning on the island, she still was not as young as she used to be, and the heat bothered her quickly, especially when she came and went from refrigerated air to none and back again.

"Sit over here, Mom." Sandy stood and took her mother's arm pulling her to the place she had secured for her. I think the breeze is better." The waitress quickly brought the drinks, and they looked at menus.

"I'm having a chocolate barnacle." Jake looked at his mom with mischievous eyes.

"First, you'll have lunch, then you can order dessert if you finish your lunch."

"I will," Jake said, and Billie knew he would. She had no idea where the pre-teen boy put so much food, but he would finish a huge lunch followed by an even bigger dessert.

****

The street where the ballet academy sat held old style two-story houses reminiscent of how the people of the time settled the Corpus Christi bay area. Large windows faced the water, absorbing the sea breeze. Leaving Sandy and her family in the front entry, Billie walked up to the desk where a young woman sat.

Billie could hear music down the hall in the otherwise quiet and pristine building. She breathed deeply the scent of perspiration and damp ballet shoes in the artificially cool air and knew the building held the blood, sweat, and tears of many dancers. Her mother had studied here, and her mother had eventually been the Artistic Director when she could no longer dance as the ballet's principal ballerina. Had Giselle regretted the child that kept her from dancing? Billie didn't think so. She knew her mother loved her and would have moved heaven and earth for her daughter. She lived the life of the prima ballerina and then lived on as a mother and teacher who helped to create more ballerinas. Giselle loved the arts whether music, dance, or whatever expression it took. She had done what she had to do to make a living, all while she made sure her daughter had the training for her own expression of art. Music.

"Excuse me," Billie said to the young woman who walked out of the door and sat at her desk.

"My name is Billie Stone. My mother used to work here as the Artistic Director many years ago. Her name was Giselle Martin." The girl looked blank.

Billie cleared her throat and proceeded. "My mother passed away recently and several of the former dancers associated with the ballet were at her funeral. I am trying to get in touch with one of them. His name is Rico Santiago—he danced with the ballet." The girl wrote down the name.

"Okay, what is your name again?" The girl spoke for the first time.

"Billie Stone, daughter of the late Giselle Martin."

Billie looked around the room at the spacious surroundings.

"I just started here and don't know many people, but I could give your information to the current Artistic Director." She shoved a pen and pad to Billie to write on.

Billie took the pen and wrote a note to a person she did not know and might never see. She put her most precious memories on a blank pad for the world to view. Giselle Martin, Artistic Director—she could not remember the dates—and she wanted to talk to Rico Santiago, a dancer when her mother was principal ballerina at the ballet. Then she wrote her cell phone number at the bottom. Would anyone see this, or would it be thrown in the wastebasket as soon as she left? She had to take a chance. She had come this far. She handed the pen and pad back to the girl who sat like a dancer, one who had been relegated to a desk—at least today.

"You'll give this to the current director?" Billie hoped her remark might prevent the potential of the trash can catching the paper as soon as she left.

"Yes ma'am, as soon as she comes back." The phone rang, and the girl hesitated.

"Thank you." Billie turned and left back the way she came. She had no way of knowing if the note would ever reach its intended target.

Chapter 34

"I've talked to my buddy, Mike, and he has agreed to take on the Montana store. I'm going to set up a satellite store here in the Corpus area. I'll see who might need IT help on the island first, and then branch out to the mainland." Neil sipped his club soda as he sat across the table from the woman in the aqua gown. He'd been eating dinner at Le Chez on the weekends when Billie sang. Most nights he could convince her to stay for a drink with him after she shut down for the evening. Sometimes she allowed him to walk her home.

"It's dark after all." He'd tried to sound convincing.

"It's Sandhill Island, after all. We don't normally have security issues. We know our neighbors."

"Well, then maybe just for the company if not the security." He'd smiled his best smile, and she had finally agreed.

"Who would I talk to about renting one of those empty stores downtown?" Neil held her arm as Billie slipped out of heels and into her flip flops for the walk home.

"Sam probably knows who owns them. It might be the Stanford Trust. They still own a lot of the island.

"Stanford Trust?" He walked beside her as she hiked her hem to step over sea grass.

"The Stanfords used to own the whole island, but

they graciously gave it back to the former owners. I wasn't around, but I guess old man Stanford was a piece of work and stole everything he could get his hands on around here. When he died, his daughter took over and created a philanthropic trust; her son runs it now. You know Meg that has the garden out behind the beautiful villa on the beach? Well, Meg and Jon run this trust, and they gave everyone on the island their holdings back. As to who owns the empty buildings? Ask Sam, he'll know. Why do you ask?"

"Well, I can live on a boat, but it's hard to run a business on a boat. I'll need an office." He guided her around the clump of grass, so she wouldn't have to step over it.

"So, you're serious about this?" Billie looked at Neil as the cloud covering the moon blew away. Neil could not believe her beauty in the moonlight—even more than in the sun.

"I am. I don't want to go back to Montana, and this area might need my help. I'm pretty handy with a computer."

"Computer nerds are always needed." Billie giggled. "So, if you're good with a computer, could you help me find someone?"

"If they have an internet presence, I can probably find them. Who did you have in mind?" They walked to the screen door of her porch which sat propped open, so Lillie could come and go. Neil heard the soft whining of puppies and a low bark.

"It's okay, Lillie, it's just me and Neil." Billie stepped up to the door of the house and hesitated. "This is a little awkward. Would you like to come in and have some tea? I'd like to discuss who I'm looking for.

However, that is the only reason I'm, uh, you know, asking you in." He could see her blush under the porch light.

"Understood. Just looking for someone online." Neil did understand, even though he hoped someday she'd invite him in for other purposes. Right now, he'd take what he could get.

Billie opened the unlocked door and walked in turning on lights. Her gown swished as she walked. The small beach house had a front entry with an antique buffet that sat just inside the door. It opened into a living room and dining room with bedrooms off each side. The kitchen was in the back. She walked immediately to the kitchen, and he followed, unsure if he should stay in the living room. Opening the refrigerator door, she took out the iced tea pitcher—a staple in a southern kitchen—and filled two glasses. Handing him one, she pointed to the living room and they walked out of the small kitchen.

"Have a seat while I change," she said walking away.

The small couch had a coffee table in front of it with coasters for the inevitable glass of tea. He wondered what else they drank on the island. He knew he could buy beer. He picked up and thumbed through a sale flyer with musical instruments just as Billie walked back through the door barefoot, in shorts and a T-shirt. She sat beside him on the couch, and a small tremor went up his spine.

"I would like to find my father," she said. "Well, at least the man I think might have been my father."

Neil stared at the woman who sat next to him on the sofa. He watched as she deftly pulled her hair back into a pony tail.

"You didn't know your father?" Neil realized how little he knew about Billie other than her mother's recent death. She had not known her father, her mother was dead, and she endured a horrible accident that took her husband and child. She faced the world alone. Did she have siblings or other family?

"No. My mother was a single parent before it was fashionable. She had been the principal dancer with the ballet in Corpus Christi, and she always said my father danced with the ballet too and couldn't marry her. When she found out about the pregnancy, she became the Artistic Director at the Corpus Christi Concert Ballet, which is the academy for the ballet. She taught three days a week while I went to school. But a man attended the funeral that I just had a feeling about. He acted like he couldn't leave Mom's urn. He stayed a long time. I decided if anyone knew him, it would be Poppy, and he did. Poppy said his name was Rico, Mom's boyfriend. I couldn't believe it. I had no idea my mother had a boyfriend. So, I talked to Sandy's mom, Martha, and she confirmed his name, Rico Santiago, a dancer. I started to put two and two together. Before the incident with the potential bonfire, I found a note, written in a man's handwriting, that said he awaited my mom's answer. I have no idea what answer he awaited, but I wondered if he authored the note. Last week I went to the ballet looking for him or someone who knew him. The receptionist took a note, and she said she would relay it to the current director. I haven't heard anything. Could you look up Rico Santiago from Corpus Christi, a man maybe in his 70s? Is that possible? I'd like to talk to him. If he is not my father, maybe he knows who is." Billie looked like she had lightened a long-standing load by many pounds after her speech.

"I can try. I'll do some looking when I get back home to my computer. Will that work?" Neil took a sip of the tea. Fresh, not the instant kind.

"Great. That's what I need. I got the feeling the girl behind the desk at the ballet might never get my note to the right person. She admitted to being new." Billie pushed back a stray hair that escaped the ponytail.

"I could look into that." He glanced at the flyers on the coffee table. "Buying a piano?" Neil picked up the flyer closest to him.

"Well, looking. After Mom died, I decided to turn her room into a music room. I used to compose, but haven't done that in a long time."

"You write music, too?" Neil had no idea why this surprised him with the amount of talent Billie exhibited.

"I used to, but it's been a long time. My therapist thinks it would be a great healing tool. Now if I had a piano, I have the room."

Neil picked up the flyer and looked at the instrument circled with a number written off the side. Pianos weren't cheap. "I hope you get what you want. I probably should leave and let you get some rest. I'll see what I can do about Rico Santiago when I get back to the computer, and I'll let you know." He stood and handed her the tea glass still half full.

"Thank you," she said as they walked out the front door onto the porch. The yellow bug light did little to keep away the flying creatures that congregated on her porch. He waved away a moth and stepped off into the moonlit night.

Chapter 35

"I'm just saying, I hope Neil can find Rico online. I would like to talk to him. If he is my father, I'd like to know, and if not, maybe he knows who is." Billie stood covered in yellow paint. The faded red hat that once said *Padre Island* had specks of yellow on it too. It was supposed to cover her hair and shade her face. It didn't do a very good job of either. The old T-shirt and shorts were equally speckled, and there were drips down her leg.

The house small; Sandy said it wouldn't take long to paint it. The women were on their third day. Billie's house would be the exact opposite of Martha's house, now yellow with white trim. Once finished, Billie's house would be white with yellow trim. It helped to have a friend who bought twice as much paint as she needed—or maybe no accident. Sandy could be devious, and she knew both houses needed painting.

"Well, I hope you find what you want. I understand wanting to know your father, but if your mom tried to keep it a secret, there may be a good reason." Sandy stepped off the short ladder that enabled her to reach the eaves while Billie painted around the windows.

"My arms ache. I haven't painted this much in years. First the music room and now the outside of the house. We deserve a break." Billie put down the paint brush and stretched her arms.

Lillie's pups were bouncing around the porch and eating solid food. In another week, they could go to their new homes. So far, Billie had only placed two of the four, but she hoped to find homes soon for the others.

"I could eat lunch. Then, maybe we could finish up this afternoon. We've only got a little more to go. Trim goes faster than the house." Sandy too rolled her shoulder and put the paint brush back in the pan.

"I made chicken salad earlier, and there's some fruit." Billie walked to the kitchen sink and washed her hands. She heard Sandy go down the hall to the bathroom.

By the time Sandy walked back in the kitchen, sandwiches were made and tea glasses full.

"When this is over, I may need more than tea." Sandy again stretched and rolled her shoulders.

"Almost done. Just keep saying that. I made you a sandwich. Sit down and rest." Billie took a bite of sandwich and sipped her tea. "Are the kids coming over today or just playing with Grandma?"

"I don't know; I left before they were up. We may owe them an evening swim or something. I've been gone the last few days, and they haven't been able to get in the water." Sandy dove into the sandwich like she hadn't eaten in days. Billie smiled and stepped to the counter and the container of cookies Martha sent. A sandwich wasn't going to be enough for Sandy with the physical labor.

****

The light breeze blew in off the ocean as Billie finally picked up the daily mail. The paint brushes were dumped unceremoniously into the trash instead of cleaning them. They had done their job well, and now they needed to be put to rest permanently. Billie didn't know when she would paint again, but when that time came, she would buy new brushes. The tiny bits of left over yellow and white paint were stored on the back porch. Martha had cooked dinner and invited Billie to join them; after a shower, she stopped by the post office before walking to Martha's for supper. There were the usual bills and junk mail and one lone overstuffed envelope—the return address said Corpus Christi. It caused a shiver up her spine as she slit it open it with her finger—cutting the skin.

Instinctively she stuck the lightly bleeding finger in her mouth and unfolded the paper.

Dear Ms. Stone,

I have found a potential employer in Corpus Christi who appreciates my ability to sell autos. I have drafted a letter—which I hope you will sign—stating that I have served my time and am once again an upstanding citizen. I'm sure a note from you would be just what the employer needs to give him confidence in me.

I am enclosing the letter for your signature. Please return it to me ASAP, and you will never hear from me again.

Sincerely,
Joe Franks
361/554-9509

Attached to the handwritten letter Billie also found a typed document with her signature line. She didn't even bother to read it. She stuffed them both back into the envelope, leaving a bloody trail on the envelope, and ran to Martha's newly painted house to find Sandy.

188

"Okay, this is too much. I'm calling the constable. Franks has to stop harassing you. First, he caused the accident. Now—even though we can't prove it—he broke into your house the night your mother died. I don't know why he is picking on you, but he has messed with the wrong family this time." Sandy yelled across the room at whoever listened as she punched 911 on her phone. Carol stood by her mother's side wide eyed as Jake's face reddened in anger.

"Aunt Billie, who is Joe Franks and why is he harassing you?" Billie looked from Sandy to Martha. Martha nodded that she should tell him.

Billie cleared her throat. "Jake, I don't know how much you are aware of the accident that took the lives of my family…"

"Yeah, Mom told us a drunk hit your car. I'm sorry." Jake looked much older than the boy who had come to the island a month ago.

"Well, Joe Franks is that man. He spent a year in jail for manslaughter, and when he got out, he had lost his job, his house, and most of his money. I'm sorry that happened to him."

"Well, he deserved it! He was drunk, and people died. A year isn't long enough." Jake, like his father, was never without an opinion.

"He made a mistake. Now he wants me to help him find a job. He blames me for his misfortunes."

"He has no one to blame but himself." Jake looked like his father, confident in his opinions and wise beyond his years.

"You're right." Billie looked at the boy. He would not be much older than her son, Jimmy, if he had lived.

"The constable is coming over to take your

statement. I don't know how much good it will do but the restraining order is back in place. So, with this, maybe it will help. Franks put it all in writing, so we know he's not that smart."

"He's an idiot. A drunken idiot!" Jake got redder by the minute.

"Okay, Jake, that's enough. We are here for Aunt Billie, but aren't going to get all riled up; it does no good. Unlike Joe Franks, we keep our heads on straight and our minds uncluttered with anger. Right?"

Jake only nodded.

"Let's take this food out on the porch, what do you say?" Martha moved to take the plates off the table and handed one to each of the kids. "Fill it up."

It wasn't long until the constable arrived to take a statement from Billie. Sandhill Island felt lucky to have constables, but they held little more power than a security guard. If things really got bad, Corpus Christi sent out reinforcements.

"Ma'am can I have the note you received in the mail?" The man in the blue uniform reached for the papers clutched tightly in Billie's hands.

"No. I mean could I bring them to you tomorrow? I want to make a copy. I have a little copier at home, and I'd like to do that before I turn them over to you."

He hesitated and then sighed. "That's fine. It can wait until tomorrow." He looked around the porch. "Thank you, and good night. I'll see you tomorrow."

He turned and left the silent porch. The only sound was the ocean on its infinite quest for the shore.

"Kids, how about an evening swim?" Sandy looked at her children as they played with their unfinished dinner. The mood for food past. They put down the plates and ran for the house.

"That's okay, I've got them." Martha stood and stacked the plates and walked into the house.

"What are you going to do with the note?" Sandy looked at her friend knowingly.

"I'm not sure yet. But I may pretend to sign it—if he comes clean about Mom's death."

"Billie. No! You've been through enough. You are *not* going to bait him. He needs to go away." Sandy's green cat-like eyes grew darker.

"I know. And I've got to stop him. He needs to confess. He killed Steve and Jimmy and now Mom. The police can't stop him, so I have to. But I may need your help. What if I convinced him to come to the island, and then I got him to confess to being in my house the night Mom died? I could wear a wire, and the police would have proof. Then he would go to jail for a long time, like he should have to begin with."

"Billie, that is really dangerous, and I don't think the police would agree to it anyway. You and I think that Franks broke into your house the night Giselle died. Raven saw someone run out the door, but she has no idea who. She could not identify him. The police don't have enough on him." Sandy took the last drink from her glass and set it on the table between them.

"That's why I have to do this. He can't get away with another murder. He thinks I've ruined his life. Well, I've done nothing compared to what he has done." Billie's eyes brimmed with tears.

"You've done nothing at all. The Texas Victim's Compensation Fund made him pay. He lost his house because of non-payment while in prison, and the same is true of his job. He's right; no one wants to hire a jail bird, but that is not your fault."

"I know. But he won't stop if someone doesn't stop him. I think the time has come that I stop him. I could tell him I'd sign only if he admitted to being in the house. If the police hear that, they have to arrest him." Billie looked at her friend as the evening sun shone through her golden hair. The women stared at each other.

"Okay, let's go!" Jake shouted, leaping through the front door with his sister behind him. They had their suits and towels and energy to spare.

"Mom, we'll be at the beach for a while," Sandy called back into the house where Martha cleaned up the dishes.

Sandy and Billie sat on the sand in shorts watching the kids bounce in the surf. The evening became darker, and Sandy told the kids when she could no longer see heads in the water, they had to come out and go home. The time drew near.

Billie breathed deeply. "I love this time of the evening. The ocean is getting ready to go to sleep. The waves become gentler as the air cools. I don't think I could ever live anywhere else."

Sandy smiled and looked out in the water for her children. "I know. I can't believe we'll be leaving in a week. The kids have to go back to school, and so do I this time. I'm really looking forward to the new job." She leaned back on her elbows and stared across the calm sea. Gulls swooped down for the evening meal. "You made a lot of headway this summer—I mean, since the bonfire incident. You are much calmer this time around. Even though I don't think it's a good idea for you to confront Franks, if you want to run this idea past the police, I'll go with you."

"You will?" Billie glanced over her shoulder.

"Yeah, I will. Maybe the police have a better idea than using you for bait. But the letter might be what finally hangs him." She stood. "I've got to get the kids in." Sandy called her kids to the beach.

Chapter 36

"It would have to be somewhere in the open—somewhere public. We would insist on that." The detective sent by the Corpus Christi police sat on the edge of the desk, Billie in the chair. Sandy stood nearby with the envelope smeared in Billie's blood. She had promised to help her friend.

"Okay, how about right after my set on Friday night? He's come to the restaurant before, and he could meet me there. I have a phone number. I can call him." Billie pulled her cell phone from her pocket and looked directly into the eyes of the detective. For once she felt confident about her involvement in bringing this chapter of her life to an end, a new feeling for her.

"Wait, let's make this a private number so he can't call you back." The detective took her phone and clicked on the settings making the cell phone number invisible to the person on the other end. "Tell him to be certain he comes after you finish on Friday night. Say you will meet him in the parking lot—or better still, how about the post office center—it's well-lit and less than a block from the restaurant. What time do you normally get finished?" The detective looked like he had done this a thousand times as he casually sipped his coffee.

"Oh, normally by 10:30 or 11:00. By then most of the patrons have gone home." Billie took the phone back from the detective.

"Okay, let's say 11:30 to be certain you're finished and to give you time to get out of the restaurant and down the block. We'll have men in place in both the restaurant and outside—along with the post office center. You make sure that the chef knows the plans—and your boyfriend."

"I don't have a boyfriend." Billie looked up at the man sitting on the desk.

"Well, the man you've been seen with lately who walks you home at night." He took another gulp of coffee.

"How do you know who walks me home at night?" Billie suddenly felt violated, her private life public these days.

The constable who had been to the house before cleared his throat. "I'm sorry, Miss Billie, but we've seen you and Neil walking home at night when we're on patrol. No one is checking into your private life, but we're patrolling the island to keep everyone safe. We've noticed he walks you home. That's a good thing, not being alone, even on Sandhill Island."

"Well, thank you, I think. Okay, so I finish my set and then walk to the post office center. When I get there, I get him to admit to breaking into my house, right?" Billie shook just thinking about the situation.

"Yes. Go slow. Don't scare him off. Be firm. You'll only sign if he admits to being in the house the night your mother died. Don't accuse him of murder or he'll run for sure. Are you sure you're okay with this? I've been told that you are under a doctor's care. The constables told me about the wreck that took your family. I'm sorry." The detective sat the cup on the desk and leaned slightly toward her.

"I am okay. I'll admit, I'm nervous, but I want to put this behind me. He won't quit until someone stops him. He's already proven that." Billie looked again at her cell phone on the desk.

"Okay, let's call him while you're here. You say he works at night, so he'll probably be home now. He'll want you to just sign the letter and mail it back. You don't want to do that. Tell him you want to see him before signing, and then he'll never bother you again. That is your line in the sand."

Billie dialed the number Franks placed at the bottom of the letter.

Chapter 37

Billie finished washing the dishes from the freshly baked cookies. She made Martha's Snickerdoodle recipe, and it turned out well. She divided them up between containers for Neil and Sam. The rest remained in her mother's antique cookie jar that sat on her counter. She couldn't remember a time when it wasn't in her house.

She stopped on the porch long enough to freshen the dog's water bowl and pet the sleeping puppies and their mother. She would miss the little rascals once they were gone, but they were getting adventuresome, and their mother continually brought them back to the safety of the porch. She knew if they were going to make good pets for someone, the time for housebreaking and training had come.

First stop—the restaurant to see Sam. With the lunch rush over, he would be planning the evening meals.

Pulling the door open to Le Chez, she smelled the fragrant scent of tomato sauce simmering and the never-ending yeast rolls as they baked. Le Chez's rolls were known far and wide. The plump chef walked out of the kitchen wiping the sweat from his brow.

"What are you doing here, pretty lady? You don't work tonight." He lightly pecked her on the cheek. He was kidding.

"Came to talk." She smiled at him and he gestured to one of the tables.

"Nothing serious, I hope." Sam turned the chair around and straddled it facing Billie.

"Well, yes and no." She placed the plastic container of cookies on the table. "I've been talking to the police."

Sam arched an eyebrow at her.

"Joe Franks sent me a letter."

"I can't believe that son of a bitch hasn't disappeared yet. Maybe I need to take care of that." He brushed his hair back with one hand in frustration.

"Well, that's what we're talking about. I'm tired of being a victim, and I want this over and done with. He wants me to sign a letter stating he's rehabilitated and not a danger to society, so he can get a better job. I can't prove he's responsible for my mother's death, but I know in my heart he broke into my house that night. I want him to go to prison for a long time. So, I talked to the Corpus Christi police, and we're setting up a sting. It will take place this Friday after my set. The police will be in Le Chez as well as the post office. We called him from the police station and set this up. He will meet me about 11:30 at the post office, and I'll be wearing a wire. I will get him to confess to being in the house the night Mom died. Then they'll move in and arrest him— once and for all."

Sam stared at her from across the table. "Are you sure that's safe? He is not to be trusted, and he has already hurt you more than once." Sam opened one button on his chef's jacket.

"The police will be there; so will Sandy, and I'm talking to Neil next. I want everyone aware of what is happening so there are no slip ups."

"I still don't like it," Sam said.

Billie slid the cookies across the table to her friend and boss. "That's where the cookies come in. They're a peace offering. Martha's Snickerdoodle recipe. I hoped to soften the blow. You are such a good friend, and I knew you would disagree with my decision, but it is one I must make. I'm tired of being a victim, Sam. I'm ready to get back to being a person again. I must get rid of Franks to do that. I'm smart enough to know I'll need help, and that is where my friends and the police come in."

"Okay, what do I have to do?" Sam looked resigned.

"I don't think Franks will even come in here, but if he does, keep an eye on him for me and let me know. He is supposed to meet me at the post office. It's well-lit and public there. I really doubt that you will even see him that night." Billie shifted in her chair.

"Okay, but I don't like it. The police better do their job." He reached across the table and took her hand. "And when this is all over, we're going to have a party at Le Chez. A coming out party for you and your new life. When is that piano to be delivered?" Sam had softened after he thought of her piano.

"Next week. I'll be paying for it for a long time. But I don't care." Billie smiled and squeezed the hand of the man across the table from her.

Sam smiled. "You'll sell so much music, you'll be leaving ol' Sam and Sandhill Island behind."

"Never," she replied.

"Well, you'll at least have that piano paid for in no time."

"That would be nice." Billie rose. "I'll see you Friday night. I need to talk to Neil, so I'll see you later." She kissed the top of his head and walked out the door leaving him at the table.

"Thanks for the cookies," he called as she walked away.

****

Neil watched the woman's hips sway the long flowing skirt as she waked down the dock. She stopped and talked a moment to Poppy sitting in the shade with his fishing pole and then continued his way. Billie was coming to visit. After all this time. She waved and pulled the strap to her bag back up on her shoulder as the sea breeze blew her hair back from her face. He pulled in the line that had not even been nibbled on that day, and set the pole aside as she walked up to his boat. The *Overboard* rocked gently in the waves made from other vessels coming and going.

"Ahoy, matie." He smiled and wondered how dumb he sounded using that old greeting.

She stopped at the edge of the boat. "Permission to come aboard, Captain?"

"Always." He tried not to look too anxious. She could still be scared off. He took her hand and helped her step into the boat. He looked around and wished he had cleaned up before she came. The small boat, normally cluttered, looked worse today. He seldom cleaned just for him.

Neil gestured to a seat on the boat. "Can I get you something to drink? I think I have water and beer, no tea."

"Water would be great." Billie sat on the bench seat, the bag at her feet while Neil disappeared into the bowels of the boat. He reappeared with a bottle of cold water and handed it to her.

"So, what brings you out today? I'm glad you decided to stop by." Neil sat down in the fishing chair and leaned toward her.

Billie reached into her bag on the floor and pulled out the plastic container of cookies. "I thought you might be starving, so I brought you these."

Neil reached for the cookies and popped open the lid. Inside crisp golden sugar cookies lay reflecting the sun from their sparkling surface. "Cookies, yum. With the way the fishing has been going today, these might be supper. Thank you. And mostly thank you for coming to visit. I've wanted you to stop by for some time." Neil looked at Billie as she straightened her skirt.

"Well, I have to admit, I had an ulterior motive for being here." She looked up at him shyly.

"Whatever the motive, I'm glad you're here." Neil immediately realized he might sound needy and clamped his mouth shut.

"I came to see you because… Well, I just left Sam's and delivered the news to him also. Sandy accompanied me to the police station this week. I received a note from Joe Franks wanting me to sign a letter for him to a potential employer. I have decided I'm tired of being a victim, and it is time Franks left me alone. The police can't arrest him for being a pain in the ass, so I'm going to get him to admit to being in my home the night Mom died. I'll wear a wire. He is to meet me after my set at the restaurant on Friday at the post office around 11:30. After that I hope to be rid of him forever. The police suggested I tell you and Sam. Evidently, they know all about me. The constables on

Sandhill Island are more observant than I knew. They have seen you walk me home at night and said I should tell my boyfriend." Billie's face turned pink at the mention of the word boyfriend. "I said I didn't have a boyfriend, but they said they meant the man who walked me home after work sometimes." She breathed deeply.

Neil remained silent for a moment as he digested the news. "That was a mouthful. You're going to be bait for some crazy? There must be a better way to go at this." Neil looked concerned and set the cookies aside.

"Well, there isn't. Like I said, he can't be arrested for what he is doing. He must do something to be arrested for—like admitting to being in my house when Mom died. The shock of the break-in caused her final stroke, but we have to get him to admit to breaking in. And that is where me and the wire come in. I told him I'd sign, but he had to come here and face me and then he could never bother me again. We made that deal on the phone."

"I don't like this. I know it is not my business, but I don't like the idea of you being in harm's way just to get a confession out of him." Neil tried not to sound confrontational, after all she finally came to visit him, but hoped he sounded concerned enough that she might rethink her plan.

"I don't see another way, and the police will be in the restaurant if he comes there, as well as at the post office. I think it will work." Billie adjusted her sunglasses as a fish flopped in the water by the boat. Shrimpers were beginning to come in, and with them, the gulls followed. Larger fish were sometimes driven closer to shore because of the boats, and then the bait fish scrambled to get out of their way.

"So, you brought me cookies to tell me this?" Neil gestured toward the container.

"My mother always said you take a gift to the host if you are visiting." Billie smiled, and Neil felt himself melting. This woman had an effect on him that he had not felt in a long time. "And to help soften the blow. I knew you wouldn't like it. None of my friends have, but they've agreed to support me because they know it is important to me."

Neil fidgeted in his seat. "If you want to do it, I'll support you. I'll be at the restaurant or the post office or both. I can walk with you if you want."

"No, I need to do this by myself. If you walk me to the post office, it will scare him off. You and the police must be out of sight. Eat at the restaurant like always, but then I'll walk by myself to the post office. and after I get the confession, the police will move in. Then you and I can walk home together or something, okay?" Billie reached for Neil's hand, and she felt like electric velvet. Her long fingers brushed over his hand and landed lightly on his. She looked up into his eyes, and he hoped he didn't look as dopey as he felt. She cleared her throat. "Do you still want to teach me to fish?" She nodded toward the water.

"I'd love to, but I don't know if they are biting today. I've hardly had a nibble all day long." Neil got up from the chair, moving with incredible slowness, afraid he would act too eager, and reached for the pole he had been using. "But first you'll have to sit on the throne—otherwise known as the fishing chair." He smiled and held the chair for her to sit in. She stood and moved to sit in the seat, and he was once again struck by her grace. She took the pole from him and sat, placing one foot on the side of the boat propped and ready for the big one to strike. Then he reached around her to show her how to cast.

Chapter 38

Neil took the pole and demonstrated the art of casting sideways and overhead. She had a choice. Then he demonstrated the button that released the line and stepped back. She looked out into the water, swung back and forward making a perfect cast, then looked up at him knowingly.

"You've done this before." Neil's eyes narrowed as he looked at her.

"Well, I did grow up on an island with Sandy's Uncle Paul."

"Paul taught you to fish, and you come in here acting like you don't know what you're doing?" Neil stood with his hands on his hips.

"Well, a little. My first love was music, and Sandy's meteorology, but we did go out fishing with Uncle Paul now and then." Billie pushed her sunglasses up on her head. Neil hovered near by. She liked him more than she wanted to let on.

The sun began its downward trend toward the water, and the shadows lengthened. Neil and Billie chatted like old friends—when a strike hit Billie's line. Expertly she pulled and wound the reel. "Get a net! We may have dinner after all." Neil obediently reached for the net and leaned over the side. The dark gray sea bass struggled to break free. Billie took the net from his hand, scooped the flopping fish from the water, and giggled when it splattered her with salty water. She picked it up by the lip and pulled the hook from its mouth. Her face radiated with accomplishment as water droplets rolled down and dripped off her chin.

"Did Uncle Paul teach you to clean it too?" Neil pushed his hat back on his head.

"Normally we let him do that for us. I hated to cut the poor things up." Billie handed the still dripping fish to Neil.

"Want to stay for supper?" Neil asked holding the wiggling fish. "We can have fish and potatoes. That's about all I've got. Oh, and cookies for dessert."

"I'd love to." Billie brushed her hair back as the sun glinted through it. She hadn't felt this free in a while. Maybe Neil was right about fishing—it could be calming to the soul. "That is if you'll clean him." She stared at the fish.

"Oh, I see; you'll catch 'em, but I have to clean 'em."

"I'll do the dishes." Billie wound a curl around her finger.

"Sold." Neil reached into the tackle box for the fillet knife and walked to the back of the boat where he cleaned the fish.

Billie held her hand up to her face to shade her eyes from the setting sun. Fish flopped in the distance, and the sun sparkled on the water like diamonds. She watched as he expertly cleaned the fish, and then washed the area free of blood. Sea gulls gathered overhead in anticipation—then dove for the morsels.

She followed Neil to the galley as he carried the fish fillets to refrigerate them. Down in the bowels of the boat sat the tiny kitchen with a half-sized refrigerator, two burner stove, and cabinets that held plastic dishes. With only room for one person, she and Neil danced around each other. He reached for the platter to place the fish on for refrigeration and hit her in the head with his elbow.

"Sorry," they both said in unison.

"The potatoes are in the cabinet behind you. I'd get them myself…" Neil pointed to the cabinet she leaned against.

Billie turned around and opened the door, staring into the dim cabinet. She saw the bag of potatoes stored in the cool, dark area. She pulled out two approximately the same size and took one step to the half-sized sink turning on the water. "Do you have a scrubber?"

Neil pointed to the cabinet underneath. Billie wondered if he scrubbed the potatoes and the dishes with the same brush.

He gently pushed her hip aside as he reached under the stove and came up with a large cast iron skillet. Then opened the refrigerator and pulled out an onion. The entire kitchen was immediately engulfed in its fumes. He peeled and sliced it, and before they were done, tears ran down both their faces. "Strong," he said wiping his face with the back of his hand. "I normally cook the fish and vegetables together in the skillet on the grill up top. Will that work for you?"

"Sounds great." Billie sniffed. "Tissues?" She wiped her hands on the towel hanging from the rack.

"Bathroom." Neil nodded behind him and continued to slice potatoes to go with the fragrant root.

Billie walked through the door to the berth. There were narrow, twin- sized beds on either side and a door at the end that had to be the bathroom. Opening the door, she found a sink and toilet with the shower hanging above them. The bathroom itself doubled as a shower. She used the toilet paper, finding no box of tissues. The manufacturer used every inch of space in a boat this size.

Two steps and back into the kitchen, she found Neil climbing up to the top. He had turned on the fan blowing fumes up and out of the hull.

Soon the propane grill smoked, and he placed the seasoned skillet on top, then went to the kitchen for the feast. Billie sat on the bench seat once again and looked out into the evening sky. The quiet sea sparkled like diamonds as the gentle waves threatened to rock her to sleep. It was a bad guest who fell asleep before dinner. She moved and stretched.

"It is a lovely evening." She smoothed her hair back.

"Yes, lovely. I'm having a beer. Are you sticking with the water?" he asked standing to return to the galley of the boat.

"Yes, thank you." Out beyond the harbor in deeper water she saw playful dolphins jump, and Paul's big shrimper came in for the evening. The dolphins and gulls followed at a safe distance.

Neil dumped the vegetables into the sizzling pan and placed a lid on top, then went back to the galley for the fish. When he returned, he placed two plates on the shelf that jutted out from the grill and checked the vegetables. He gently placed the fillets in the pan and sprinkled some sort of seasoning on the fragrant food as it cooked. The fish would cook quickly.

Billie could not imagine a more perfect evening. Clouds formed in the distance, and the setting sun sprayed through them with fingers of gold.

He handed her a plate and fork and sat beside her on the bench, their legs touching.

"How's the fish?" He took a mouthful and nodded to her plate. "Aside from Mike, you're the first guest this bucket of bolts has had the pleasure of hosting."

She took a bite and savored the light delicate flesh that almost melted in her mouth. She hadn't fished since a young girl and could not remember if she ate her own catch then.

"Wonderful. Maybe I do like to fish after all. It's just been a long time, and I'd forgotten."

Neil brushed the hair out of her face and looked earnestly at her. "What do I have to do to talk you out of baiting Franks?"

Thunder clapped in the distance, and Billie looked up.

"You can't. I have to take back my life. I would feel better if you were there that night, along with the police. You have a calming effect on me."

"I do? Because you make me jumpy as a schoolboy."

"I didn't mean to," she said around another bite of fish and vegetables wondering if she could duplicate this dish in her own kitchen, or if it required a boat and sunset.

"I think that is the thing. You don't try, I just melt. I melted the first time I saw you walking toward the post office. I think you were wearing that same skirt. I loved the way it swayed in the breeze."

The conversation had taken a personal turn. She reached for the bottle of water as he reached for his drink, and they brushed hands. The sky began to darken as the clouds rolled in.

"Looks like a storm. We may get wet," Billie said looking into the distance and forking another mouthful of fish. "Hurricane season is right around the corner."

"Yep, looks like a storm." He closed the cover to the grill leaving the skillet inside and then sat back down on the bench to finish his supper just as big drops of rain plummeted the deck of the boat.

Grabbing plates and drinks they ran for the safety of the galley as the grill sizzled in the rain. Once inside Billie turned on the water over the sink to wash the dishes. Neil's arms folded around her and nuzzled her neck.

The tiny kitchen felt on fire, and she turned to face him. His eyes looked down her face and neck and then back up. He leaned in to gently kiss her lips as thunder boomed overhead, and she jumped. He turned off the faucet behind her and pulled her closer. She melted into him. She felt a passion that she thought had died years ago and kissed him back as they tugged at each other's clothes. Desperate to be rid of them, they stumbled to the tiny twin-sized bed in the berth and fell into a heap as clothing shed. His hand slid down her hips, and she unbuttoned the wrap-around skirt. Standing, she let the skirt he loved so much fall to the ground. She climbed back into the bed and reached for his zipper. He sighed as she slid it down, warm flesh pulsing beneath it. He expertly unhooked her bra with one hand while pulling off her panties with the other and somehow, they ended up under the bedspread that covered the tiny bed.

Later in the dark Billie dozed in his arms as the boat gently rocked and rain splattered up top. She had not felt this warm and safe in a long time. She felt like the young woman she used to be, before the terrible accident that changed her life. She snuggled against his chest as he brushed the hair from her face—the storm continued.

"I guess you'll need to stay the night. It's dark and raining. Do you think the constables know where you are?" He spoke in the dark.

"Probably, it's a small island." Billie snuggled deeper into his body as he drew her in and soon both were snoring in the tiny bed.

Chapter 39

Sandy sat on her mother's porch until the rain drove her in. The kids were finishing their baths and getting ready for bed. Earlier she had walked to Billie's and found her not home. Poppy sat on the porch partially under the swing next to the dogs when she walked in.

"Poppy, is Billie here?" She saw he had the black puppy in his lap stroking it gently as the mother licked another one clean.

"No, Miss Sandy. She's on the boat with Neil. I saw her go there, and then when it looked like it might storm, I came to take care of the dogs. That's okay, isn't it?"

"Of course, it's okay. That's going to be a great looking dog you've got there, when he grows up. He's cute as a button now." Sandy leaned down and stroked the dog's nose, then looked out toward the water. Billie was on the boat with Neil. She had seen this coming but wondered if her friend would ever warm up to another man after Steve. She only hoped Neil would be good to her. She had been through enough in one lifetime. She felt sure Neil was a good guy.

"I might just stay here until Miss Billie gets back." He placed the dog back with his mother and the litter. Tiny grunts could be heard as it burrowed its way under the litter mates and found a warm, comfortable spot.

"Good for you, Poppy. I'm going to go home and leave the dogs in your capable hands. Good night." She walked away back toward her mother's home.

"Good night, Miss Sandy," she heard him say over her shoulder.

****

Billie waited until she heard the unmistakable motor that pushed Paul's shrimper out past Neil's boat the next morning. She knew he saw her on the boat last night and didn't want to discuss it. She felt happy, and if she knew Paul, he'd be happy for her too, but still she didn't know her feelings for Neil. She wasn't sure yet what last night meant.

Neil fixed her toast and eggs for breakfast while she maneuvered in the tiny shower—and then presented them to her up top in the morning sun.

"I need to get home. I assume Poppy took care of the dogs last night, but I do need to leave." She rinsed her dish in the tiny sink; then he filled it with warm water to soak the plates.

"Can I come by later? We still haven't discussed how Friday night will go." He pulled her into an embrace.

"Of course. I'll be home. They're to deliver the piano this afternoon and tune it." She pulled away and turned toward the steps leading to the top of the boat. Once more he grabbed her hand and held it to his lips, then let her go.

It turned into a glorious morning. She climbed up on the dock and walked toward home. Poppy sat in the shade with his pole already in the water. She needed to talk to him and probably thank him for helping her out last night.

213

"Good morning, Poppy." She walked toward him and pushed her sunglasses up on her head.

"Good morning, Miss Billie. I took good care of the dogs last night." Right to the point. It made her smile.

"Thank you. I knew you would. "So, you named your dog Blackie?"

"Well, since he's a boy and black, I thought I'd name him Blackie. I always liked that name for a dog, what do you think?"

"I like it. He'll be a good dog for you. Blackie. It has a nice ring to it. Would you like to take him home today? He and his brothers and sisters are six weeks old, so it is time they went to their new homes." Billie looked at the older man who had been on Sandhill Island as long as she could remember, and he suddenly looked like a kid. His smile so wide it showed spaces where teeth should be, he stood up.

"Today? Really? I have his bowls and food and a bed, and everything all ready. I can really take him home with me today?"

"I think it is time. They're bringing my piano this afternoon, and I thought, if you took your pup and Carol took hers, I could move Lillie and the two remaining pups to the back porch—at least until the delivery is finalized."

Poppy stood, instantly reeling in the line on his pole and stowing his fishing gear. They walked to Billie's house together and chatted about the glorious morning.

"Well, Lillie, will it be okay if Blackie goes to live with Poppy? You'll still see him all the time. He can come back and visit anytime." Billie knelt and rubbed the mother's head as Poppy held his pup.

"I'll take real good care of your baby, Lillie, and we'll come visit a lot." Poppy kissed the top of the dog's head and walked away talking gently to his new companion. The mother whined softly watching them go. Lillie stood and watched from the porch, and then licked the remaining pups, circling to find a place to lay once again.

Billie's phone rang in her pocket. It said "Sandy."

"So how was your evening?" Sandy's voice taunted her in a friendly manner. "I came by to see you, but Poppy said you were on the boat with Neil."

"I had a wonderful evening. I caught a fish. And yes, I did spend it with Neil." Billie twirled her hair like she used to as a child.

"I'm really glad to hear it, girlfriend. He's a wonderful guy, and you two are lucky to have each other."

Billie knew Sandy would not give her trouble over her impromptu dinner date.

"But I really don't know what it meant. We haven't discussed it."

"That's okay, isn't it?" Sandy's kids could be heard in the background.

"Yes, it is, for now. By the way, I just gave away the first pup. Poppy took his dog home with him. Does Carol want her dog now and is that okay with your mom?" Billie walked in the living room and through to her mother's old bedroom. She stood considering the blank space and envisioned her new piano gracing its floor.

"I'm sure she does' let me ask Mom first, though. I'll get back with you. By the way, are they bringing the piano today?"

"This afternoon. I'm standing in the music room now thinking about how to arrange things." Light shown in the window with its new curtain, and shadows flowed to the side of the room where the burn had once been. It could no longer be seen.

"What time did they say it would arrive? My kids want to go swimming."

"They just said this afternoon. You know how delivery people are. I wanted to try to move the dogs to the back porch before the piano gets here. What do you think?" Billie absently rubbed her toe over the invisible burn on the floor.

"Maybe a good idea. Let me talk to Mom, and then I'll get back with you. Talk to you later." Sandy clicked off, and Billie opened the closet door to review her music once again all in place on the shelves, when someone knocked on the door.

In the entry that stood open Neil leaned on the door facing.

"Good morning again. I hope I'm not too early."

Billie reached for his hand to pull him through and again, he kissed her fingers.

"No, you're not too early. You can help me actually; I want to move Lillie and her pups to the back porch before the piano gets here and scares them all to death." Still holding his hand, she guided him to what would soon be the music room. "What do you think? I realize you never saw it before, but Paul did such a great job refinishing the floor, and it has a fresh coat of paint and look…" She opened the closet door to display her music in order on the shelves.

"Very nice. I hope to hear music coming from here

soon." Shadows played across his face as leaves blew in the ocean breeze outside the window.

"You will. I'll play something just for you." She pulled him near, and he kissed her gently.

"I found Rico Santiago for you, and I sent him an email telling him you wanted to meet him. I guess I did that right?" He looked into her dark eyes that showed surprise.

"Yes, of course, I want to see him. I suppose I didn't realize it would happen so soon."

"Well, he still has an email at the ballet, but I think he is semi-retired. I hope he gets it. After the luck you had at the ballet the day you went into Corpus Christi, he might not."

Billie sighed. "Well, now, I guess we wait?"

"I guess. I also have an address and phone if we need to go that route. Who knows if they're current, but we can try. Now about the dogs."

"Yes, I don't know when the delivery will be this afternoon, but I can pick up the pups and call Lillie if you bring the bedding. First, though let's make sure there is a place on the back porch where she won't be disturbed. I'll leave the door shut until after the piano is in place. I can always move her back afterwards." After surveying the back porch and finding a place beside the dryer, Billie walked toward the front with Neil behind her. She leaned down and picked up the puppy that had the bad luck to end up on the top of the pile and folded him into her chest, then reached for the second. Lillie stood and looked questioningly at the woman who fed her.

"It's okay, Lillie. We're taking you and the pups somewhere quieter for the day, and then we'll bring them back later. It is going to get a little noisy with deliveries running in and out." She patted the dog's brown head as she talked and soothed her stress. Lillie stood on hind legs nosing her babies as Neil handed Billie the final one.

"Come on, Lillie. Come on girl." Billie coaxed the velvet-coated dog to follow her and the wriggling bundles Billie clutched to her chest. Lillie had never been in the rest of the house; she preferred the screened porch and salt air.

Neil placed the bedding by the dryer and then stepped back. Billie lay the pups on the familiar bedding and opened the window above them as Lillie made countless turns round and round before finally settling in. She then began the arduous job of washing each of her babies one more time.

After opening the rest of the windows on the back porch, Billie closed the door between the porch and kitchen to give the family that curled up on the rags by the dryer time to rest, then walked to the front. Neil sat on the front porch looking out to sea.

"You have a tremendous view here." He said without looking up.

"I love it. I wouldn't want to live anywhere else. Sandhill Island is my home." She placed a hand on his shoulder, and he instinctively covered it with his as noise rounded the corner.

"She's sleeping in my room! She's my dog!" Carol's voice carried as she walked with her brother and mom to Billie's house. She rounded the corner in her swimsuit and flip flops, towel draped over her shoulder.

"No fighting at Aunt Billie's or you'll go back

home without a swim." Sandy's voice. She followed her children. She appeared with a big floppy hat on her blonde hair and a cover up over a swim suit. Jake brought up the rear, head down and towel in hand.

Billie put her hand over her mouth to hide the smile. "So, you're swimming today?"

"Hi, Aunt Billie," Carol said and walked onto the porch and then gasped. "Where's my dog?"

"It's okay. She and her family are on the back porch for a little while. We moved them because my piano is to be delivered today, and I didn't want them to be scared or in the way. You can go see them." Billie gestured toward the house, and Carol wasted no time running through the door to the back porch. Her brother right behind her.

"Hi. My family just barges in like they own the place." Sandy walked onto the porch and sat her beach bag down. "We're going swimming this afternoon, and then I thought we might take the pup home with us tonight. Give her a little time away from Lillie before we stick her in the car and drive to Biloxi. Mom said it would be okay. How are you two?"

"We're fine." Billie squeezed Neil's shoulder and he smiled. "So, Martha thinks the dog can come live for a few days at her house, huh?"

"That's what she said. When I left, she was digging through old rags to make a bed." Sandy held her hand up to shade her eyes and looked toward the road. "This might be your truck. We're heading for the water and will get out of the way."

Sandy trotted through the house as the truck pulled into the yard of sand and sea grass. The petite grand piano would become a permanent fixture in the tiny beach house. It would probably never be moved again.

Billie waved as Sandy and her kids ran back out the front door and toward the beach. Jake complained about wanting to stay and watch. Of course, he would also complain about missing the swim if he stayed, and Sandy didn't want him in the way. There were always choices in life.

Chapter 40

Looking in the mirror, the old man tied his tie with arthritic hands. He'd read the email. He could check ballet email from home—and he hurried to get ready. The man said he sent the note for Billie, and Rico wasted no time. He would go before she changed her mind. He might be foolish just dropping by without calling first, but he had learned not to wait for the things that were important in life. He wanted to see his daughter. He knew where she lived; same place as her mother. Sandhill Island. He had been there often enough but never allowed to see Billie. He'd pleaded with Giselle, but she was emphatic that Billie not think she had a father who could not or would not live with her.

He walked out the door of the aging apartment that sat down the street from the ballet and started the rusty car. It caught on the second try. Salt air could be hard on vehicles, so he seldom bought new. An old car worked fine for his needs and fit his personality. He didn't need new-fangled things with GPS and options he didn't know how to use anyway. He smiled as he looked in the rear-view mirror. He hoped she liked him once she met him. She had to. After all she was his daughter, but he felt nervous.

Pulling up at the ferry, he waited until the flat boat that took cars and pedestrians from the mainland to the island made its return trip. The few cars leaving the island rolled off the ferry, and the few going the other direction pulled on. Once they were parked, the ferry made the trip to the island.

It took him no time to find the tiny beach house that Giselle had loved so much. Recently painted white with yellow trim, it looked to have been kept in good repair. He slowed as he drove past it the first time, circling the island and getting a feel for the changes that had happened. The harbor was in good shape, with new marinas, and the downtown stores had tourists coming and going. Business appeared to be good. He drove past Le Chez—he knew the restaurant where Billie sang. There were a few cars in the parking lot, but maybe it held more on the weekends. He knew he wasted time. He'd come this far, and he needed to complete the mission.

Circling back toward her house, he passed a man walking to the harbor in a T-shirt, shorts, and flip flops he didn't look comfortable in. Tourist. Islanders wore them from birth. The man walked down the newly built dock in the direction of a few boats that were tied up. Some tourists lived on their boats, he knew, even though it must be close quarters.

Rico pulled up at the beach house and cut the engine, stepping out into the afternoon heat. The door to the screened in porch was propped open with stones, and beautiful music flowed out the door and every open window in the house.

He rapped on the door of the porch first, and a dog lifted her head to give him a low growl. She lay on a pallet on the floor under the swing that had been raised. She had a litter of puppies with her.

"Hi, doggie. Is Billie home?" He heard the music stop and a bench move across the wooden floor. He knocked once again. "Anyone home?" he called, but not too loudly. He didn't want to disturb the dog any more than he already had.

Footsteps moved in the house, and then he saw the woman who moved like Giselle only with dark hair. He had seen her at the funeral but decided not to introduce himself that day. Emotions were already too high and control fragile.

She walked barefoot in shorts and moved like a dancer. He knocked again, and she looked up. The dog growled once more but made no movement toward him.

The young woman stood in the open door to the house and stared his way. He couldn't see her expression with shadows inside the house, and he had no idea if she recognized him. But then, why would she? She had never seen him before—he didn't think. She stood still and then walked toward the door.

Rico cleared his throat. "Good afternoon." He took off the fedora and leaned on his cane.

She walked toward him and once again a low growl came from under the swing. "It's okay, Lillie," she said as she walked slowly toward the man outside her home.

"Rico? Rico Santiago." It was a statement more than a question.

"Yes." His voice cracked. "I'm Rico Santiago from Corpus Christi. I'm...a friend of your mother's."

She stepped out onto the porch, looked him up and down, and then smiled her mother's smile. His heart melted. "I saw you at the funeral. And I believe you were more than a friend to my mother." She reached a hand out to shake his, but he took it and brought it to his lips. She smelled of lemon oil.

"I received an email from your friend Neil, and I came as fast as I could. At my age, waiting is not an option." He smiled, and the dog sat back down with her pups. The older man and younger woman stared at each other in awkward silence.

"Would you like to come in?" Billie gestured to the open door. "I think I have some tea made."

She ushered him through the entry to the couch that sat in the living room, then trotted off to the kitchen. Rico looked around the room he had not been in since Giselle told him not to come back.

Billie sat a tray on the coffee table with drinks and cookies and handed a glass to him.

"Rico Santiago. You came. I wondered if the email would sound like a come on or something when Neil said he contacted you. I can't believe you came." She looked him over as he sipped the iced tea.

"I've always wanted to come, but your mother thought it wasn't a good idea. So, I stayed away."

"So, you're still working with the ballet? Your email came from them." She crossed her legs and pushed her hair behind one ear.

"Well, my name is still affiliated with them. I don't dance, but I do work part time in the office and at certain times when they need me. Actually, I still live just down the street from the school. And I understand you sing at Le Chez here on the island?" He posed it as a question knowing the answer.

"Yes, on the weekends. Like you, I'm part time. I moved here after the accident that took my family. I came to heal, and then Mom got sick and eventually died. Now, I'm just beginning to do the healing. In fact, I got a piano. I ordered it from a place in Corpus, and they just delivered."

"You play as well as sing?"

"Yes, I compose. That's why I needed the piano. I think it will be good to get back into it. I haven't done it for years." Billie sipped the tea and sat it back on the tray.

"That sounds wonderful. Will you play for me?" His leathery face wrinkled even more when he smiled.

Billie hesitated. "I can play something from my set at the restaurant. I haven't written anything yet." She rose and offered her hand. He struggled into a standing position with the aid of the cane, and she led him into her mother's bedroom—now her music room.

Rico walked to the entrance of a bedroom he had been in before, and his heart felt suddenly in his throat. He would not tell his daughter Giselle had allowed him here. In the center of the room sat a petite baby grand piano in gleaming mahogany shining in the sun. Obviously recently polished, it shone like a new penny and smelled of lemon oil. Over in the corner sat a turquoise winged back chair that once graced Giselle's living room. Billie led him to the chair, pulled out the bench seat she pushed under the piano when not in use, and sat down.

Her fingers glided over the keys as though a part of the instrument, and she began, slowly at first, Billie Holiday's *God Bless the Child*. Her voice reminded him of raw honey dripping from the comb as it slowly gave up its life and fell to the ground. When she finished, she turned to see him wiping away a tear he had promised himself would not fall that day. Not in front of the daughter he had never known until now. She would not see him as weak.

"Incredible," was all he could murmur without the flood of tears that threatened to fall.

She stood and walked to his side and kissed him lightly on the head, and he folded her in an embrace.

Chapter 41

Slipping into sandals that lay by the bed in the sun, Billie wriggled her toes in the warmth. Sandy should be here any moment, and they had an appointment at the police station. She wanted to go over one more time the agenda for Friday night.

"Anyone home?" Sandy called as she walked in the front door that normally stood open allowing the sea breeze to blow in the house.

"Hey, lady. You ready?" Billie walked from the bedroom into the small living room where her friend stood.

"You bet. The more we go over this the better I feel. The military taught me to first brief and then to debrief. I want to know what's going on. I may make a checklist."

"You do that. I just want it to be over." Billie grabbed her purse, and they walked out the door together closing it behind them. "Lillie, you're in charge. Take care of things, and I'll be back soon." Lillie lay back down on the pallet with her babies and sighed.

"You really want to do this?" Sandy pushed her blonde hair back from her face and looked at her friend with green cat-like eyes.

"It's the only way. It's time I got my life back. He's taken enough. If I just sign the letter he'll be back

227

again when he needs something else. He must confess to being in the house with Mom the night she died. The DA said if he confesses, he can be held on breaking and entering and manslaughter. He should go to prison for a long time."

"You're putting yourself in danger to get a confession out of him. I think that's a job for the police."

"Like I said, they can't hold him unless he does something or confesses."

The faded red Honda pulled into the front yard, and the door opened. Raven stepped out in shorts and a baseball cap. She seldom wore anything but scrubs for her nursing job.

"Raven!" Billie ran to hug her friend. "I thought you were going to meet us at the police station." She wrapped her arms around the woman who had been like a sister to her when they both looked after Giselle. Raven then turned and squeezed Sandy's shoulder.

"Well, I thought I might get a look at the puppies, but I'm running behind. Maybe we can do that after?"

"Of course. Come on and walk with us. You know how close everything is around here." The women walked out of the yard and down the road to the tiny brick building that housed the constables who looked after their island. Two police cars sat in the only parking places. There would have been nowhere to park if they drove.

The door opened to a small office—no waiting room. Nothing ever happened on Sandhill Island. They didn't need much space. The scent of stale coffee and newspapers that littered the desks in the other room flowed through the room. A box of petrified doughnuts sat open on the desk like a shrine. A young woman manned the reception desk, but no introductions were needed. The detective from Corpus Christi rose from the back and ushered in the three women.

"Have a seat," the detective gestured to folding chairs next to the commandeered desk.

The door opened once again, and Neil walked in, taking off his sunglasses and looking around. String's head automatically ducked to be sure of clearing the door facing, and Sam walked in last, still in his chef's jacket.

"I see you brought your entourage." The detective smiled.

"My friends are concerned about Friday night," Billie replied. More folding chairs appeared as if by magic.

"Okay, here's the plan. Billie is to finish her set at 11:00, and then, after casually changing her shoes and taking her purse, she will walk to the post office. The way is well lit. My men will be in the parking lot of Le Chez, and the post office, in unmarked cars looking like a normal tourist. One will be in the restaurant. There's no way he can get past us, and no way for a slip up. Ms. Stone will wear a wire, and she will talk to Franks at the post office. She will tell him she'll sign the letter only if he states he broke into her house the night of her mother's death. After we hear that, we will move in and arrest him."

"Okay, about the wire. How does this fit and what do I wear? I normally wear cocktail dresses to perform in." Billie fidgeted in her seat.

"We'll have a female officer there to help you get fitted for the wire. It fastens in your bra. I don't know what your dress looks like, but the more coverage the better."

"Maybe the black one? It has wider straps and you could wear the jacket with it." Raven spoke for the first time since walking in the door. Having lived with Billie for so long, she knew her clothes better than anyone.

"Yes, I don't have to wear a strapless bra with that one." Billie shifted in her seat and Sandy put a hand on her shoulder.

"I'll help you out, honey." Sandy tried to be a soothing effect on Billie.

"The important thing is to make sure you don't deviate from the norm. Don't change how you normally dress; it could draw attention to you, and we want this night to be just like any other."

"Well, I normally change up what I wear as often as possible. I don't think this will draw attention."

"Good. Okay, everyone knows what they are going to do, right? Just be cool, and do what you normally do. But Billie is to walk alone. Anyone with her might scare Franks off. We don't want that. The police will be watching her all the time, and she will be wired. So, please, don't interfere. We'll take good care of your friend." The detective sat as usual on the edge of the desk he had taken over with the perpetual cup of coffee to his lips.

Neil cleared his throat. "I normally eat at Le Chez on Friday. Sam will be there too, as will String."

"I'll be around," Sandy chimed in with no indication of where she planned to be, "and Raven too."

Raven nodded.

Billie couldn't wait to get this over with.

Chapter 42

Friday finally came.

Sandy planned to leave for home on Saturday morning and promised the kids one last swim in the ocean. Billie wouldn't miss this for the world. It might be months before her friends came back.

"I can't believe you're leaving tomorrow." Billie brushed the sand from her toes and leaned back on her elbows watching the kids play in the water. They got along better now than when they first came to the island, and she realized she'd watched both grow up this summer. They had stayed for months instead of weeks because of her. Sandy—the best friend ever.

"I never intended to stay this long, but I'm glad I did. We had time together. I had time with Mom, both houses got painted, Carol picked out her puppy." Sandy rubbed her hand down the damp puppy that lay exhausted on the towel beside her. It had been playing in the water's edge with the kids until just a moment ago. "I think the kids are getting along much better than when they first came, don't you?" Sandy picked up the commuter cup with coffee and raised it too her lips, watching her son do handstands in the salty water.

"I know. Do you think something in particular happened, or did they just grow up some?" A crab walked toward Billie, and then stopped looking up at the intruder. She sat on his beach.

"I think part of it is that they were away from home, stuck together without other friends and the electronics. Jake had limited electronics, so he had to join the real world." She waved at her daughter who held up the star fish with one hand and rubbed salt water from her eyes with the other.

"You ready for tonight?" Sandy took another sip of coffee.

"As ready as I'll ever be, I guess. I just want it over."

"Me too, girlfriend. The kids will be tucked into bed early tonight at Mom's and I'll be at Le Chez."

****

After a shower and something light to eat, Billie slipped into the black stretchy dress with wide straps. Raven was right, it might be better to wear a bra with straps; she was unsure how the wire fastened inside the bra. The long flowing shear jacket lay on the bed. She slipped it on. She could wear it with most of her dresses, and she reached in the closet for black pumps to sing in. She would carry them to work as usual. Picking up the black evening bag, she walked toward the front door and out onto the porch, closing the door. She needed this behind her.

Raven had taken her pup home with her earlier in the week. Billie began to feel badly for Lillie. Only one baby left. She wondered if dogs mourned the loss of their babies.

The one little puppy crawled over his mom and tugged on her tail. After tonight, Billie would be more concerned with finding it a home. She leaned down to pet Lillie good bye.

"Okay girl, I'm off to work. You and little bit stay

here, and I'll see you later, okay?" Lillie thumped her tail in agreement, and the pup jumped at her jacket as it flowed in the breeze.

Billie slipped into her flip flops and stepped off the porch, heading to work.

****

Franks rolled the rusted sedan off the ferry and slowly drove around the island. He had time on his hands. He knew she never finished until after eleven, and she said she would meet him at the post office at 11:30. That gave her time to finish and walk the short distance to the postal center where the islanders picked up their mail. Smart. The place well-lit and visible to the public. He wasn't going to let her get away this time. The car dealership said they were interested in him, and he would not let this job get away, even if it killed him. His life needed to get back to normal. He'd done his time, and now if society would let him, he'd be a fine upstanding citizen once again.

He drove past the mansion that sat on the water's edge, and once again marveled that anyone would spend that much money on a house so close to the water. But the gardens were well tended. A woman in a faded dress and ragged sun hat worked pulling weeds as the sun went down. She looked up and waved. He waved back.

The dock was well lit even though not quite dark. He guessed the winter Texans didn't relish falling off the dock into the water at night. He watched a man climb out of a boat called *Overboard* and walk away down the dock. He paused to talk to a bum sitting with his fishing pole and dog by his side. More people with money.

He drove past the post office and into the tiny town. Shops were closed, but tourists still wandered down the sidewalks. He parked the car in the shadows in front of one of the shops, and then waited. He could see the post office from here as it became dark. No one would notice him, and he could wait until he saw her approaching before he left the car. The time was ripe, and his luck about to change. He pulled a sandwich from the brown paper bag and popped the top of the soda can. Once he landed the sales job, he could quit brown bagging it.

****

Carol lay in her bed, fresh from the shower. Mom said goodnight and left to see Aunt Billie one more time before leaving in the morning. Carol wanted to go too, but Mom said they were to be in bed early tonight, so they could leave in the morning. Her new puppy lay on the floor by the bed on the towel Grandma gave it for a bed—and whined. Mom said not to let it in bed with her, but the puppy acted so sad. She probably missed her mom and litter mates. Carol squatted down and picked up the puppy cuddling it to her and crawled back in the bed. Mom would never know, and the puppy would be happier.

The bed pushed up against the open window; a light breeze blew in. Carol could hear the ocean waves, not like at home where the windows were closed and the air conditioner running. It felt cooler at home, but Carol loved Grandma's bungalow by the ocean. The puppy snuggled and continued to whine.

Carol reached for the bedside table and the hand mirror that once belonged to Giselle and showed it to her puppy. She talked softly showing the puppy her

234

reflection but still it cried. It had been fed and had gone outside to pee. Why did it cry? Then Carol wondered how she would feel if someone took her away from her family. In the morning, they would go back to Biloxi, and the pup would go with them. They might not see Lillie again for months. Carol quickly slipped out of bed and put on the clothes laid out for morning, then slid her feet into the new pink flip flops. Back up on the bed she unhooked the wooden screen and grabbed her pup and the mirror. She'd take her to see her mom once more before leaving. She'd hurry, and no one would ever know she left. She'd be back before Grandma knew she'd gone.

With the screen unhooked, she could easily climb back in once she got home. She ran with the puppy tucked under her arm still holding the mirror, her two favorite things in the world. The night felt heavy with humidity, but the moon appeared from behind the clouds most of the time. She knew the way to Aunt Billie's, even in the dark.

Struck with a sudden urge to pee, Carol made a detour toward the post office with public bathrooms. Mom said always go to the bathroom before going to bed at night, but she couldn't remember if she had that evening. Anyway, she knew where the bathrooms were. She'd stop on the way to Billie's and then they'd see Lillie one last time.

****

The crowd seemed normal for a Friday as Billie and String performed a medley of blues music. She had a note on the piano with the order of songs. She felt like shaking things up a little tonight. She didn't think she would be so nervous, but it helped her sooth her mood.

She surveyed the crowd and saw no sign of Franks. She didn't think he would come to the restaurant tonight.

Neil sat at the table with Sandy, and they talked like old friends, each watching the restaurant with furtive glances. Sam stuck his head out on the deck and surveyed the crowd several times. A man Billie didn't know sat in the dark corner alone eating shrimp and drinking water. The waiter came by several times, but he waved him away. Probably one of the undercover cops.

The evening was muggy; the guests were thinning out. The sea breeze did not blow away the humidity tonight, and tourists weren't used to it. Sam often made better profits on drinks on nights like this. Tonight, would be no exception.

The man in the corner finally paid his bill and stood to leave. That was the signal. The guests were mostly gone except for one table of tourists who had more than their share of alcohol. Sam would see they got home. Very few drove to the restaurant anyway.

Billie signaled String, and they finished. She thanked everyone for coming, then began putting away the mics. The bus boys rolled the piano inside. Billie walked past the table where Neil and Sandy sat and said good night to them, then headed to the bathroom.

Inside she found a woman she had not seen before.

"Ms. Stone?" the woman asked in a husky voice.

"Yes," Billie said with a start, then realized she talked to the undercover cop.

She held up a tiny wire and after checking the stalls she locked the door.

"Nice dress. This should be easy enough to hide. You want to take off the jacket, and I'll help you get this settled where it's not too uncomfortable?"

Billie slipped off the jacket and lowered the zipper that ran up the back of the dress. The officer had done this many times, as evidenced by her quick action. The wire quickly put in place under the bra strap, the cop zipped her back up.

"Okay, don't be nervous. We're all around you. Just change your shoes, pick up your purse like normal, and begin a slow walk toward the post office. Smith, did you hear that?" The officer held a finger to her ear and nodded. "He got it. You're good to go. No sweat." She nodded approval and unlocked the bathroom door.

Chapter 43

Billie walked to the kitchen where she'd left her flip flops and purse. She nodded to Sam and String who stood talking in the kitchen. Changing her shoes, she walked out the kitchen door and into the dining room. Bus boys were cleaning tables and stacking chairs to mop the floors.

Neil and Sandy stood in the back near the piano with drinks in hand. She wondered if they had drunk anything since walking in the door. They appeared to still have the same glasses she'd seen for hours.

Billie opened the restaurant door and stepped into the night once again. She could hear the ocean's relentless rush to the shore. No tourists tonight. She looked up and saw clouds rolling across the moon, causing occasional shadows. In the distance, she saw the post office with its lights aglow, and she could see the heavy mist begin to fall. Her dress clung to her stiff legs as she walked toward the light. Time to finish this.

****

The sandwich and soda long gone, Franks thought about a bathroom. He knew about the one at the post office. Did he dare use it now? Already 11:00 and the bitch should be done soon. He'd walk that way and see what happened. He could wait. He stepped out of the car with creaking doors and started toward the post office when he saw her—the little girl often with

Billie—not her daughter, but a niece or friend's daughter? She carried something in the crook of her arm. Why would a kid be out alone this time of night? The little girl walked to the bathroom door of the post office and pulled the door open with one hand holding on to a puppy with the other. She would be good insurance. Just in case the bitch decided to renege. His bathroom needs long since forgotten, he walked toward the women's restroom and pulled open the door. The little girl stood in the middle of the room talking softly to the pup.

****

"I think I just saw Carol going in the bathroom." Billie talked softly hoping someone would hear her. "A young girl who looked like my friend's daughter just walked into the bathroom. I don't know for sure. Can you hear me?"

It was a rhetorical question. The police could hear her, but she could not hear them. She had to know, and she walked as slowly as possible toward the bathroom at the post office.

Pulling open the door she found a man bent over and talking to someone. A large rolling bucket sat in the middle of the room with a mop sticking out. It must have been left by the cleaning crew. He turned and looked at her. Franks stood talking to Carol who shook, hugging the pup to her chest. A man in the women's bathroom could be unnerving.

"What are you doing with her? This is the women's bathroom." Billie tried to remain calm knowing the police heard everything said.

"Well, Ms. Stone, we meet again. I just asked this little lady if she knew you, and it seems you are her aunt."

"She's not my aunt, we just call her that." Carol's voice shook.

"Carol, hun, you should take your dog and go home. Mr. Franks and I need to talk." Billie hoped Carol would do as she said and not be scared.

"I just wanted to take her to see her mother one more time." Carol shook even more and looked like she might cry. She knew this conversation wasn't normal.

"Okay, honey. Go home, and I'll bring Lillie to see her." Billie reached around Franks for Carol's arm—and he stepped in front of her.

"No, I think she'll stay for now." He reached into his jacket and retrieved the paper. "I think she'll watch her Aunt Billie sign the letter, and then maybe I'll let her go."

"You can't do that. You can't use a child as leverage. It's kidnapping." Billie tried to remain calm. Surely the police heard her. The wire in her bra felt like a boulder and sweat ran between her breasts. She knew if the wire remained, the police knew how things were going. And it definitely remained.

"Well, sign the letter, Aunt Billie, and your little niece can leave." Franks' eyes narrowed as he looked Billie up and down.

Billie could take it no more. "Haven't you hurt enough children? Let her go!" Billie lunged for Carol and shoved Franks out of the way. He fell into the stall and struggled to get up.

"Run Carol! Run!" Billie shoved the girl and her puppy out the bathroom door. Then grabbed the mop handle and swung as hard as she could as Franks attempted to stand. It connected with his arm with a loud crack. Then she kicked over the bucket of soapy water. As she slammed the door behind her, she heard him hit the ground. She hoped the slick floor slowed him down some. She dialed 911 as she rounded the corner of the building that led to the backside. Where were the police?

"Aunt Billie?" A tiny voice called from the alley.

"Carol! Why didn't your run honey?" She grabbed the girl's arm and pulled her along.

"I didn't know where to go," she sobbed.

Billie looked behind her. The child still clutched the mirror she gave her and the tiny puppy. She had to hide her before Franks found them both.

"Be very quiet." Billie put a finger to her lips as she talked and slunk along the side of buildings, then ran from place to place trying to hide. They ran behind buildings, peeking out each time before slipping to the next, then crossed the street and the empty lot where Meg used to sell her vegetables. Then they ran for the house. She could still hear the 911 operator asking for her location. Afraid Franks was right behind her, she remained quiet.

She held on tightly to Carol's hand, and the girl kept up the pace even with her hands full. She had young legs. When suddenly Carol stopped, jerking her hand loose. Billie turned around. She found the girl reaching for the mirror that lay on the ground reflecting the moon as it slid out from behind a cloud. She had dropped the mirror that she loved so much. The puppy, still clutched tightly in the crook of her arm, whined softly.

Billie grabbed the mirror with one hand and the girl with the other and then sprinted toward the house she grew up in, the same house her mother died in, and the one Billie tried to set afire. She stopped, hiding beside the one tree in the yard, and instinctively looked behind her. The moon once again covered its face with clouds, and Billie felt safe enough to move on.

"Carol, I want you to hide when we get to the house." She looked both ways and then ran for the house. "Now go! Take the puppy and hide!"

She watched as the girl ran for the end of the porch where she got stuck during the bonfire issue when her brother had to rescue her. She slid like a lizard under a rock as Billie ran for the porch. The screen door was propped open for Lillie and held in place with the stack of large meditation stones. She almost reached the inside door—before being brutally knocked down. The mirror slid from her hand, and she heard breaking glass. Seven years bad luck, she thought, and then wondered why that idea would come to her at a time like this. And where did Lillie and her puppy go? Surely the dog would help her.

****

"I can't hear a thing, Detective." The constable sat in his own car with the Corpus Christi detective. A light drizzle began, but they didn't want to use the windshield wipers and draw attention to the parked cars.

"Well, that's because she's not talking." The detective sipped his coffee.

"I saw the little girl go in the bathroom and now I don't know where Ms. Stone is. She walked this way, and suddenly she just disappeared. I don't know, maybe she needed to go to the bathroom."

"I haven't heard water running. I think this whole

night is a waste. He's not coming. He'd be stupid to come to the island where she lives. If he wanted this to work out, he'd insist she come to Corpus."

"I haven't heard anything in some time. I wonder if the wire is working." The constable adjusted the binoculars and looked from the women's bathroom to the post office and back again.

"We'll wait a few minutes. It is early. She'll show up." The detective once again sipped the tepid drink.

****

"I knew you'd come here. You're so predictable. You think I don't know where your house is?" Franks held her down on the floor of the porch with his body weight.

"Of course, you do. You were here the night my mother died. You're the reason she is dead." Billie shook under the weight of the man who had ruined her life.

"Yea, I was there. The old witch tried to get away. Then she fell off the bed. Serves her right. All I did was ask where you were. I didn't kill her."

"You caused her death, that's manslaughter." Billie's voice sounded like a little girl's, and she hated that.

He grabbed a handful of her hair and roughly jerked her head backwards. Her neck strained at an angle, and he leaned down like a lover to whisper in her ear. "This didn't have to go like this. I just wanted your help, and you treated me like scum. Now I don't think it's too much to ask for your signature on the letter I wrote, do you? Sign it, and I'll leave you and the little girl alone."

He dropped the paper in front of her without ever

letting go of her hair. The letter said she knew him to no longer be a threat to society. He deserved a second chance. Nowhere did it mention he had killed her family or caused Giselle's final stroke. How many chances did he think he got? She shook with fear as tears streamed down her face, and her nose ran onto the paper he thrust in front of her. She lay face down on her own front porch, once again a victim of Joe Franks.

The splintered mirror in front of her again reflected the moon rising out on the ocean as clouds parted. And then she saw it. The face of fear. The reflection of a face pained and scared and looking more immature than the little girl who hid under the porch awaiting Billie's rescue. The eyes were wide and frightened—and victimized. She hated those eyes—hated being a victim—and she looked away. The screen door, held open with the stack of stones her mother loved, were within reach. The meditation stones that were supposed to help her heal were useless tonight. Or maybe not.

Letting go of her hair, Franks sat back, fumbling in his pockets for the pen with his good arm, the letter in front of her. She twisted and knocked him over—the stones fell to the ground and the door slowly began to shut. She grasped the largest stone and swung with all her might. He fell sideways grabbing his previously injured arm. The black dress slid almost up to her waist and she didn't care. Modesty had no place here. She jumped on top of the man who had caused her so much pain in life and again slammed the stone into his head. Then, as she raised her arm to bash his head in, something grabbed her in mid-arc.

"No, Billie. Not like this." She struggled to break free. She had him! She would put an end to this once and for all. But she found her arm held tightly—and reality began to surface. She slowly realized the voice belonged to Neil.

The lights and sirens in the yard were all around. Once again, she was lifted from a prone position by strong but gentle arms, the arms of Neil and the constable. Franks lay in a puddle of his own blood on her porch. She felt certain he was dead. He would not be coming for her again. And then he moved.

"Aunt Billie?" The tiny voice called her again. Carol. Safe? She sounded the same as the day of the fire. Billie turned around. Carol stood with the wiggling puppy still in the crook of her arm, her face smudged and dirty. A soft warm body pushed itself into Billie's arms. Lillie licked her face, and then ran to her pup. Carol held the baby to its mother for comfort.

There were people all over her porch and house. The constable and detective were asking her questions, Neil stood behind her protectively as the paramedics looked her over. Franks was placed in handcuffs, even with a head gash and possible broken arm, and led away. String showed up with Sam and Raven; then Billie saw her. Sandy pushed her way through the crowd to her best friend.

"What happened?" After a big hug, she sat down on the floor next to the chair Billie had finally been convinced to take, and pulled Carol into her lap. Lillie once again nosed her pup, and Sandy rubbed her ears.

Billie found her voice shaky, but she could talk. "Franks followed Carol into the bathroom to try to get to me. He had a letter to a potential employer, and he wanted me to sign it. He not only caused the wreck, he also caused Mom's final stroke. He said so. But he still wanted me to help him."

"Ms. Stone, your wire quit for a while. Could be the moisture or something, but we did get the confession. Maybe when you fell, it jiggled something and started working again. I have it on tape." The detective hovered over her as she told her story.

"I thought you couldn't hear me. I said several things I thought would bring you running. So, I dialed 911 as I ran. I never did finish that conversation."

"That's okay, they get that all the time." The detective tasted the coffee once more and walked to the door, dumping it on the sand outside. "With the confession, we can charge him with manslaughter, breaking and entering, and attempted kidnapping of the little girl in the bathroom. With his history, we should be able to make it stick."

"Thank you, Detective, thank you all." Billie leaned her head back against Neil, and he brushed her hair out of her eyes.

Martha and Jake pushed through the crowd to Sandy's side. She had called them after everything happened, knowing they might be aware of lights and sirens.

Suddenly a tiny warm body slid under Sandy's arm to its mother, sitting at Billie's feet. The final puppy. Where had it been and had Lillie been looking for it when the melee hit?

"That little fella spoken for?" The constable reached down and picked up the puppy as Lillie tried once again to bathe it.

"No, but he'd make a great police dog, don't you think?" Billie smiled at the cop who had continued to look for her when the others had not.

"Yes, I do. Can I have him?"

"What do you think, Lillie? Okay if your boy grows up to be a policeman?" Billie patted the head of the dog who had been with her through so much, and Lillie smiled her doggie smile.

Epilogue

Gentle breezes blew across salty water, then through Billie's long dark hair. She sat on the bench seat next to the galley, hoping to not get her white sundress and sandals soaked. Mom always loved the dress on her. She said it reminded her of the pinafores she wore as a child. She wasn't a child anymore.

The brass urn in her lap reflected the sunlight, and an occasional drop of water rolled down its side. Her mother had loved the sea. When Giselle left the ballet to have her baby, she picked Sandhill Island for the beach. She said it freed her soul.

Rico, in the linen suit he wore to the funeral, adjusted the white fedora to shade his eyes. His cane rested on the floor of the boat, his gnarled hands placed on the top. Neil helped him to a seat, after he had seated the women. Billie turned to find Poppy standing on the dock. She waved, and he returned it with a salute.

What would she do without Neil? He had offered to take them out to scatter the ashes. He had learned so much since the first time she went out on the water with him. He had a great teacher. What would she do without Poppy and all the people of Sandhill Island? They were a community—a family—and they looked after each other.

Pulling away from the dock, the *Overboard* plowed through the wake of another vessel coming in. The boat rocked slightly, and Billie, her mother's urn in her lap, looked out to sea. Gulls flew overhead, waiting on mullet to come to the surface or scraps to be thrown over from fishermen. The circle of life. One organism died so others could live. Much like Billie and Giselle. Even though Joe Franks had not personally killed her mother, she died because of him just the same. If Franks had not broken into the house to find Billie, he wouldn't have threatened Giselle, causing the final stroke. But, Giselle had died, just like Steve and Jimmy. Billie was left to carry on.

The bottle green ocean at the dock quickly became navy blue as the boat headed out to deeper water. They would meet Paul at his normal shrimping place and then spread Giselle's ashes. They were the people who had known and loved Giselle, they and one newcomer. Billie knew she would have loved him too. Neil understood her pain. He had been through the death of parents and the ending of a relationship and understood moving on.

"She was the most beautiful woman I ever knew." Rico spoke first. No one on the boat had anything to say since leaving the dock. He gazed at the urn that held the remains of his lover. "If I hadn't had responsibilities elsewhere…," He trailed off and stared out to sea, then back at Billie, wiping a tear from his eye. "I had a wife and children, and your mother wouldn't let me break the family up. I could have been a father to you also, Billie, but your mother said no. I hope you understand. I loved your mother. I also loved my wife and family, and they had to come first."

"I understand, Rico." She placed her hand on his arm. Maybe someday she'd get around to calling him

Dad. "I wish I had known you earlier too, but I had a good life with Mom. She provided a wonderful home and loved me very much. I had only one parent, but I had a great one. I also had Martha." Billie nodded to the woman who sat across from her in the blue dress.

"You were easy to love, sweetheart. You and your mother both. Now that things have changed, and Giselle is gone, we still have each other."

Billie saw the shrimper in the distance. Neil pointed the nose of the boat toward the ship that sat idle and waiting. Once within a safe distance, he stopped the boat. Paul and his workers stood on the deck of their ship and waved. Billie waved back. Then they all stood at attention, the water like glass as evening approached.

Billie stood first. Taking the top off the urn, she moved to the back of the boat. "I love you, Mom," she said simply and tipped the urn, emptying ashes into the ocean. The gray dust floated on top of the water. When she turned, Martha stood next to her with Neil at her elbow to steady her in the rocking boat. She handed the urn to her mother's friend. Martha ceremoniously sprinkled a portion of the ashes on the water as she whispered under her breath then walked back to sit.

Rico took the urn from Billie and clutched it to his chest. "I loved you always," he said, sobbing, "and I'll take good care of our little girl." He brushed away a tear that oozed under his sunglasses and rolled down his leathery cheek. In turn he sprinkled part of the ashes, the ocean receiving them impatiently. Rico handed the urn back to Billie. Leaning on the cane, he wobbled back to the bench.

Inside the urn there remained some of the ashes of the woman they all loved. Billie couldn't take them home, as much as she wanted to. Her mother belonged to the sea. She spilled the last of the ashes over the side watching them float, then filter down to depths only the ocean understood. Neil instantly appeared beside her, taking her hand and bringing it to his lips, gently kissing fingers that had just held the urn.

"It is a beautiful thing you just did. Your mother would have been proud." Then he kissed her lips and led her back to the seat as she held the urn in one hand.

The sweet sunlight of evening shone on the calm ocean. Birds rested, floating on the surface as the sun began to sink. A golden glow covered the water as well as the sky; sea birds dipped silently down for their supper in the ethereal quiet, reminiscent of a church.

Gulls screeched as Neil started the engine of the *Overboard* and turned for the dock and its home on Sandhill Island.

A word about the author…

Peggy Chambers calls Enid, Oklahoma home. She has been writing for several years and is an award-winning author, always working on another. She has two children, five grandchildren, and lives with her husband and dog. She attended Phillips University, the University of Central Oklahoma, and is a graduate of the University of Oklahoma. She is a member of the Enid Writers' Club, Oklahoma Writers' Federation, Inc., and Oklahoma Women Bloggers. There is always another story weaving itself around in her brain trying to come out. There aren't enough hours in the day!

Peggy writes a weekly blog that you can find at http://peggylchambers.wordpress.com/ Like her on Facebook at https://www.facebook.com/BraWars, or connect with her on Twitter at #ChambersPeggy.

Thank you for purchasing
this publication of The Wild Rose Press, Inc.

If you enjoyed the story, we would appreciate your
letting others know by leaving a review.

For other wonderful stories,
please visit our on-line bookstore at
www.thewildrosepress.com.

For questions or more information
contact us at
info@thewildrosepress.com.

The Wild Rose Press, Inc.
www.thewildrosepress.com

Stay current with The Wild Rose Press, Inc.

Like us on Facebook

https://www.facebook.com/TheWildRosePress

And Follow us on Twitter
https://twitter.com/WildRosePress